The author is a retired detective chief inspector and former head of Brighton CID. He was the senior investigating officer on many murder investigations. He operated in the UK and Ireland with the Counter Terrorism Command. He was recruited into the Security Service (MI5) Counter Espionage Department, working in the UK and USA with the FBI. As a young detective inspector, he was involved in the interrogation of Argentine Commander Alfredo Astiz during the Falklands War. He has a BA degree in history and politics and is a keen photographer. He also owns and manages a woodland in West Sussex and is an enthusiastic motorcyclist.

To my three darling girls: my wife, Jill, and daughters, Clair and Cheryl. During my career I worked long hours and was often away for extended periods of time. Home was my sanctuary, and I always looked forward to their love and happiness. Thank you.

George A Smith

A SECRET EXISTENCE

AUSTIN MACAULEY PUBLISHERS™

LONDON • CAMBRIDGE • NEW YORK • SHARJAH

A CIP catalogue record for this title is available from the British Library.

ISBN 9781398412163 (Paperback)
ISBN 9781398412170 (ePub e-book)

www.austinmacauley.com

First Published (2021)
Austin Macauley Publishers Ltd
25 Canada Square
Canary Wharf
London
E14 5LQ

Chapter One
The Introduction

Silence follows the death of an agent. Killed whilst on active service is a problematic inconvenience. The UK Government does not comment on reports of members of the security services killed on active service. Their identity and exploits will remain unknown to the public. No recognition of their sacrifice will be acknowledged or published. Honours awarded will remain behind closed doors. The security of the State is paramount: operations will continue.

The train from West Sussex arrived at London's Victoria Railway Station at 7 am. It was a pleasant, warm summer Sunday morning in early June. In contrast to a normal working day, there were few passengers alighting from the train.

Julian Lawson stepped onto the platform and walked briskly across the concourse, depositing his neatly folded Sunday Telegraph in a rubbish bin. He was on official business. It was, therefore, appropriate for him to be wearing a dark-pinstriped suit, white shirt and a formal tie.

As he walked towards the main exit he momentarily paused, looked up at the station clock and glanced at his own wristwatch whilst discreetly looking around to ensure he was not being followed before heading into the Palace Road.

His appointment was for 9 am. He had arranged to be there at 8 am to collect the classified brief and prepare for the important meeting. In accordance with departmental policy, he did not carry a briefcase or any official documentation. The location for the meeting was a fifteen-minute walk away, allowing him time to slow the pace and enjoy a stroll through this pleasant and historic part of London SW1.

Lawson was a senior member of the Security Service (MI5). It was responsible for protecting the UK—its citizens and interests at home and overseas—against threats to national security and was responsible to the Home Office. Its sister organisation, the Secret Intelligence Service (MI6) works on suppressing and countering threats from abroad and was responsible to the Foreign Office. The two organisations often work together.

He turned right and continued the short walk towards Buckingham Palace. The Royal Standard was flying over the palace signifying the queen in residence. At the imposing black tall iron gates, he paused to look across the courtyard to watch, in the distance, two guardsmen on sentry duty marching to their points. The public pedestrian area in front of the palace was spotlessly clean and the pavements still damp from the recent water spray from the road cleaning machines.

Early morning in summer is the best time to be in London, before the hordes of noisy tourists arrive discarding their burger wrappers and empty drinks cans. Long ago, Lawson decided he did not like crowds. He thrived in a busy working environment but, when off-duty, he sought the peaceful quiet country life and enjoyed outdoor pursuits. He was quietly confident of his own ability and politically savvy. However, he did not enjoy social gatherings with strangers to simply engage in small talk or gossip. He had a polite smile and was courteous but, in recent times, rarely laughed or showed outward emotion.

The huge main black wrought irons gates to the palace, emblazoned with the United Kingdom's Royal coat of arms in green and gold, were open but with tight security in place. A retractable metal anti-terrorist barrier was positioned across the entrance. Several uniformed police officers were present behind the barrier, each wearing a ballistic vest and clasping a Heckler & Koch semi-automatic carbine in the challenge position. In addition, each wore a holstered Glock 26 pistol and a webbed belt on which was fitted a canister of incapacitant CS gas, handcuffs, a baton and communication equipment.

The guardsmen in their bright red tunics, parading in the background, are the ceremonial face of Great Britain. The armed police at the gate represent reality.

Lawson walked across to the gleaming white marble edifice of the Queen Victoria memorial, positioned grandly in front of the palace. He stood on the steps looking up The Mall to Admiralty Arch. The day was dawning with a clear blue sky. Tall London plane trees, lined either side of the wide straight avenue, gently swaying in the early morning breeze, accompanied by the tapping sound of loose lanyards flapping against the columns of flagpoles. The London plane is one of the most iconic tree species in the city. Its exact origins are not known, but most likely a hybrid between the American sycamore and the majestic Oriental plane.

Few vehicles were travelling down The Mall with only a spattering of black London taxis and the occasional embassy limousine. Early morning joggers joined them. He thought: *Likely to be staff from nearby royal and diplomatic establishments, plus the occasional multimillionaire rock star from nearby Birdcage Walk.*

The previous day, The Mall had been an avenue of pageantry, pomp and splendour with the Sovereign being escorted by the Household Cavalry from Buckingham Palace to Horse Guards Parade for the Queen's birthday parade at the Trooping of the Colour. The asphalt road surface of The Mall, for the half mile from Admiralty Arch to the gates of Buckingham Palace, is coloured oxide red to give the effect of a giant red carpet.

The Mall follows the course of an old path at the edge of St James's Park and was laid out in the reign of Charles II. In the 17th century, it was London's most fashionable promenade.

Lawson remembered this fact with a sad smile. The last time he stood there was two years earlier with his wife. He had acted at 'her tour guide', jokingly, explaining the history of the area. He had then taken her by the hand and together 'promenaded' and skipped up the middle of The Mall, much to the amusement of motorists. Earlier in the day, they had joined the large crowd cheering the Royal Family on the balcony of Buckingham Palace and he had taken photographs of the Battle of Britain Memorial Flight, flying low down The Mall.

It was the last time they had visited London together: A much-treasured memory. Six months later, she died from cancer at age thirty-four. She had been a much-admired schoolteacher. They had been married for ten years and had plans and dreams to last a lifetime. He thought about her constantly but rarely spoke about his loss. Since her death there had been no other relationship. At the time, he had been a detective chief inspector seconded to the Counter-Terrorism Directorate.

Now he was a member of Britain's Security Service, more commonly known to the public as MI5. As was the practice, he operated under a cover name. Friends and relatives back in Sussex did not know the true nature of his employment nor the identity under which he operated.

Stepping from the Queen Victoria Memorial, Lawson crossed to the left side of The Mall and continued walking, stopping only to allow a silver Range Rover to cross his path and turned into the gated precinct of Clarence House. He thought with a grin: *Possibly Prince Charles collecting his Sunday newspapers.*

On reaching Admiralty Arch, he crossed in front of the building and onto a paved side road. Checking that no one was observing his movements, he approached a small oak door at the side of Admiralty Arch and rang the bell. There was no number or signage on the door. A small portal opened at eye-level and he offered his ID card. To the uninitiated it had the appearance of a bank card but, when scanned by the appropriate equipment, it displayed on screen the bearer's photograph and authenticating details.

The door opened. He entered and was met by a middle-aged—physically imposing man in a well pressed grey suit and highly polished black shoes. Lawson thought: *Retired Military Intelligence. Non-commissioned. A good man to have in a tight spot, no doubt.*

"Good morning, sir. Trust you had a pleasant journey. Please follow me. You are the only appointment for today. The subject has left his home address and is en-route here."

They walked to the reception desk where Lawson was handed a sealed heavy-duty envelope marked: "Secret. Only to be opened by SO/2A."

On the reception desk sat a computer and a telephone. The only other furniture was a brown leather two-seater chesterfield. It was a smallish room with a high ceiling and several round windows three metres from the ground. The appearance was of a government building, but with an absence of any pictures or notices.

It was the interrogation suite for MI5. A stranger entering the building would be at a loss to identify its function, or the department it represented.

"The Hardy Room has been set-up for you," said the man.

"Will you require A/V recording and a colour facial photograph?"

"Yes please. Also, ensure immediate forensic examination of his mobile phone and any other electronic device he has with him."

Lawson was escorted along a short corridor to the Hardy Room. It was one of the four identical rooms in the complex. Each named after a famous naval commander. When not occupied, the rooms remain locked. The Receptionist opened the door using a swipe card. Lawson entered and the door was closed behind him.

Lawson sat down on a comfortable leather swivel chair behind a large military desk. He imagined both had been requisitioned from the office of some long departed First Sea Lord. In front of the desk were two upright chairs and a small round coffee table. Again, no pictures or notices adorned the magnolia painted walls. A laptop computer was positioned on the desk to his right and activated into life by swiping his "ID card".

He opened the sealed envelope and took out a purple-coloured folder marked "Secret. Operation Forest Wood." He had no prior knowledge of the case. This was not unusual. At home, the previous evening Lawson had received a brief telephone call from the duty desk asking him to conduct an interview.

In this line of work, the abiding rule was to preserve security and integrity: You only ever knew what you need to know in order to do the job. You never asked for, or gave, more than what was required. Rarely did an individual know the complete picture of an operation: If one element of the structure failed, the rest would remain sound.

Lawson read the brief. He assessed he would need about an hour to achieve the desired result. The folder also contained the subject's CV and other relevant documentation.

The telephone rang.

"Sir, the subject has arrived and I have placed him in the waiting room. One mobile phone submitted for examination."

"Thank you. Give me ten minutes and then bring him in."

Lawson tapped the computer screen into life and keyed into a covert view of the waiting room. He sat back and watched his subject.

The man remained standing. He was wearing an ill-fitting—light brown anorak and appeared uncomfortable. The walls of the waiting room were bare except for a government Health and Safety poster. Rocking and moving slowly from one foot to the other, the man stood reading the poster for a

13

few moments before walking to the other end of the room and back for a second look at the poster. Sitting in the only chair, he began straightening his tie and patting down his hair before, once more, getting to his feet to again read the poster.

Lawson closed the screen. There was a knock on the door and the Receptionist entered with the man. No introductions were given.

He removed his reading spectacles and placed them in his top jacket pocket. "Please," said Lawson gesturing to the chair in front of his desk.

The subject held out his hand. Lawson remained seated and allowed the silence to continue. The man sat down.

"You were invited here by a letter marked confidential. It directed that you bring it with you. May I have it please?"

The man took the letter from his inner jacket pocket and handed it over.

"Sorry, I missed your name."

Lawson glanced across the desk.

"I didn't give it."

He took the letter and placed it in the folder in front of him.

"The letter directed that you should not communicate details of the visit with anyone. Have you?"

"No, I haven't."

Lawson took a single sheet of paper from the folder.

"Mr Marsh, I note you are a married man with two teenage daughters. Ten years ago, you gained government employment as a driver and, until six months ago, worked at the Central Carpool in London. Did you drive for any of the big chiefs?"

"Many, including two prime ministers."

Lawson tapped the computer and studied the screen, which was not visible to Marsh.

"Yes, I see, and also cabinet ministers and senior figures from the military."

Appearing to relax his stance, and with a smile, Lawson continued.

"Spending time with them on long journeys, and chatting with other drivers, you must have got to know much gossip. Any interesting stories to tell?"

"Lots, they're certainly not a bunch of angels," he responded with a laugh. Then realising the situation, he added, "Of course, I remain discreet at all times."

"When you joined government service you signed the Official Secrets Act and were security vetted?"

"Yes."

Lawson continued to refer to the computer screen.

"And I see over the years you have attended 'refreshers' to be updated on your security obligations. Six months ago, your role was enhanced. How would you define your job?"

Marsh laughed at that suggestion.

"Now, I'm a more senior dogs-body. I often do the longer 'drives' which involve overnight stays. I get to carry their luggage, press their suits and anything they tell me to do. I even end up sorting out birthday presents for their loved ones."

Lawson detected bitterness in the man's voice, but let it pass.

"And the occasional trips abroad?"

"Yes, to Brussels and a few other places."

Marsh then paused and appeared annoyed.

"Look here, who are you? The letter only had an HM Government heading with no department name, telling me to phone a number. When I did, some woman told me to come here. There was not even a name of the sender, just some unreadable squiggle."

Lawson did not address the query or attempt to offer reassurance.

"Last month, you accompanied a cabinet minister and his team on a four-day visit to Moscow. What was your role?"

Marsh fidgeted in his chair.

"I know what you are getting at. I was Mr Invisible on that trip. Little Miss Snooty had it in for me."

Leaning back in his swivel chair, Lawson looked directly at the man.

"Please explain."

"I was the odd-job man, carrying their luggage, collecting and delivering all sorts of things and even up at three in the morning ironing suits. I was the invisible man as far as they were concerned. The minister never spoke to me. His private secretary, little Miss Snooty, gave the orders in her posh Oxford educated voice, 'Thingy do this or that', she never used my name or said thank you."

Lawson sat forward as though offering understanding.

"You clearly feel you were not appreciated on that trip. How about other trips?"

Marsh continued to fidget.

"The only time I get to sniff the inside of a Jag is if I'm driving. Otherwise, it is being squeezed into the back of a people carrier with the luggage or at the back of a plane with a pack of sandwiches, whilst the minister and little Miss

Snooty turn left for first class treatment with champagne and caviar."

Lawson thought: *A dangerous man to have in this position* He said nothing and gestured for Marsh to continue.

"Has little Miss Snooty reported me for being rude to her? OK, slap me on the wrist and I promise not to be a bad boy again."

Lawson did not reply immediately. He studied Marsh, and then leaned forward slightly.

"Before you embarked on the Moscow visit, you attended a security briefing and were warned about the dangers of street crime and being targeted by the Russian Security Service." Lawson did not seek a reply.

Intending to catch Marsh off balance, he introduced a low-ball.

"How long have you been having an affair with your neighbour's wife at number twenty-six?"

Marsh stared straight ahead. He appeared taken aback and remained silent.

"Mr Marsh, I am not here to moralise on your matrimonial arrangements. The question was posed to demonstrate we know a great deal about you."

Lawson maintained his gaze on Marsh.

"My organisation exists to protect the security of the UK. I do not apologise if my questions upset you. Be under no illusion, we do not act on rumour or suspicion, but on facts. I demand the truth. When the government team arrived in Moscow, some of the staff, including you, were booked into the tourist Hotel Cosmos. You were allocated room number two hundred and six."

Marsh interrupted.

"And I obeyed the security briefing. I had no visitors."

Lawson raised his hand indicating Marsh to stop.

"Let me continue. After dinner on the first evening, you left the hotel for a stroll in Red Square. Then to a café and had a beer. Then another. Being away from home can be lonely. I can understand that. A blonde girl smiled, and you invited her to your table for a drink. What happened next?"

"We had a couple of drinks and then I went back to the hotel alone."

Lawson retained his calm path of questioning.

"Mr Marsh, she invited you back to her flat and you made love. Then you went back to your hotel alone. I know what happened, but I require you to tell me. Please continue."

"She was lonely. She had only been in Moscow for a couple of weeks: On a business course learning English. This is embarrassing. I went back to her flat to look at her English study books and we ended up making love. That's it."

"And what did you tell her about yourself?"

"Only that I was with the UK team."

Lawson softened his tone, but clearly demonstrated he was in the driving seat.

"And you visited her flat the next night. After making love, what did you talk about? Please be specific."

"Ah, I joked about little Miss Snooty and the others but nothing secret. OK I was indiscreet, but no harm was done."

"And you have agreed to meet her when she visits London?"

"God, you have done your homework. She hopes to come over this summer for a holiday and we have arranged to spend a couple of days together. We just clicked. I'm very fond of her."

Lawson leaned forward with both elbows resting on the desk.

"Barry, she is a prostitute."

"She isn't. She never asked for a penny from me."

"No need, the Russian Security Service is her paymaster. Remember what I said earlier: We don't operate on rumour only facts."

Lawson sat back in his chair.

Marsh wiped his perspiring forehead.

"I don't believe you."

"OK, let me be blunt." retorted Lawson.

He gently tapped on the desk as he made each point.

"You are fifty-two years of age. Overweight with a receding hairline. If I may say, not a stylish dresser or a man with money. You are not a 'good catch' for an extremely attractive long-legged—twenty-two-year-old Russian girl seeking her fortune in the West."

Lawson keyed into the laptop and viewed the screen.

"When you entered this building, your mobile phone was taken from you. Does anyone else use it?"

"No."

"And you had it with you in Moscow?"

"Yes."

Lawson pressed a silent buzzer just below the desktop and continued viewing the screen. There was a knock at the door and the Receptionist entered and handed him a sealed transparent exhibit bag. He held it up.

"Mr Marsh is this your mobile?"

"Yes."

"On the 28th May, where were you?"

"On the Moscow trip."

Reading from a report attached to the exhibit bag, Lawson continued.

"Forensic analysis of the mobile shows that at twenty-three fifty hours, local time, on 28th May it was opened and fitted with a sophisticated miniaturised tracking device and bug. This will require more detailed examination."

Gaining direct eye contact with Marsh, he continued.

"So, at the time you were with your lover and had your trousers off, someone borrowed your mobile and 'upgraded' it. Mr Walsh, you were targeted by a hostile intelligence agency, i.e. Russia. And you took the bait."

Marsh clinched his fists in anger.

"This sounds like James Bond stuff. Surely the Cold War is over and—"

Lawson interrupted him.

"The names may have changed, but the game remains the same. Information is power: It gives the holder an advantage on political, economic and military issues. You refer to yourself as Mr Invisible. In their eyes, your position makes you an asset for collecting damaging and useful information on ministers, military personnel and government business. The same operatives who removed your mobile would have filmed the love making sessions. Blackmail is a powerful and destroying tool."

Marsh closed his eyes and began to bite his knuckles.

Lawson continued.

"Fortunately for you, we quickly identified the sting and only little damage has occurred. Had the relationship continued, you would have been drawn deeper into their net. Favours would have been requested, for example, gossip on ministers, and then blackmail and pressure to acquire more sensitive information. You are a silly, but lucky man. A few months down the line and it would have been Special Branch knocking at your door with the likelihood of disgrace in the media and prison."

Marsh wiped away tears from his cheeks.

"What is going to happen to me?"

Lawson opened the folder and took out various documents.

"You will resign your position and not discuss your actions or this meeting with anyone."

He passed across the desk a prepared letter of resignation and a separate letter acknowledging his indiscretions in Moscow.

"Please read and sign both. Subject to your continued cooperation, this will remain our secret."

Marsh signed both and handed them to Lawson.

"What shall I tell my wife?"

Lawson replied, "I suggest you say the travelling was too much and you wanted a change of lifestyle."

He took from the folder a P45 and handed it to Marsh.

"Your termination of employment starts from now. You will not go back to your office nor contact any member of staff. Tomorrow, two months' salary will be paid into your bank account. You will be monitored and if we need to speak with you again, we will initiate contact."

The door opened and the Receptionist entered. Lawson remained seated and nodded towards the door.

"Good day, Mr Marsh."

Marsh left and the door was closed.

Lawson clicked the computer screen back to life and watched the subject leave the building. He then switched off the computer and closed the folder.

A few minutes later there was a knock on the door. In walked a woman holding two mugs of coffee

"Good morning Julian, I'm Felicity Moorcroft, Foreign Office. I watched your interrogation from the Monitoring Room."

She sat down and placed a mug of coffee in front of him.

An educated and confident individual clearly at ease with her surroundings, thought Lawson.

"Thank you. Interrogation? No, that was just a gentle interview with a pathetic individual. The script rarely changes. It was the classic 'honeytrap' operation: older fat man goes abroad and is flattered by the attentions of a much younger beautiful girl and he closes down all his senses and is convinced its love."

Moorcroft smiled.

"What is your assessment of him?"

"He's damaged goods. With his attitude, he should not be around ministers. A word of caution, I assess him a suicide risk."

Lawson signed off the file, placed it in a sealed envelope, and handed it to her.

She placed it in her briefcase.

"MI5 working on a Sunday. Must be double-time for payment."

He laughed.

"For queen and country: No charge."

With an equal smile she responded.

"Thank you for doing this. It is appreciated. There was an urgent need to disrupt further contact. The young Russian lady is scheduled in the UK soon. A welcoming party is being arranged."

In accordance with policy, they left the building separately.

As Lawson walked back down The Mall, he mused: "Felicity Moorcroft, Foreign Office? Not her real name and, no doubt, she is with MI6. What a complicated web we weave. I do not know her identity and she does not know mine. Even my mum has never heard of Julian Lawson. I've been operational with the organisation for three months and don't know the identity of any of my colleagues – and none of them know my true background."

As he strolled towards Victoria Railway Station, his thoughts went back to his MI5 recruitment and training some months earlier.

Chapter Two

The Recruitment

Four months earlier, Lawson had operated in a different environment and with a different name: His correct birth name was Ben Swan. He had been a serving police officer with only a vague knowledge of MI5: A career detective operating in the CID and other specialist departments within the service. For the previous two years, he had been a member of the Counter-Terrorism Directorate operating throughout the UK and with frequent visits to both Southern and Northern Ireland.

The BA internal flight from Belfast arrived at Heathrow Airport on time at 7:30 pm. It was a cold damp Friday evening. The main terminal was crowded with business passengers keen to get home for the start of the weekend.

Detective Chief Inspector, Ben Swan, strolled towards the airport's police station secure car park and climbed into his Land Rover Defender truck saying quietly:

"Hello, old girl. I'm knackered; let us go home for a peaceful weekend." It was his first day off in two weeks. He removed his tie and unbuttoned the top of his shirt.

He started the engine, pushed open the primitive front two air-vents on the dash and switched on the radio.

"Let's have some soothing classic FM."

Progressing slowly through the heavy evening traffic, he made his way down the A3 and onto the quieter A283 and then south towards his hometown Petworth. He was now driving through the pleasant countryside of leafy West Sussex and would soon be home.

Swan enjoyed driving his faithful Defender truck. His wife had called it his "Tonka toy". It was fifteen years old, but the basic design had not changed much since the introduction of Land Rovers in 1948. The diesel engine was noisy; the heating system basic, with a comfortable top speed that did not exceed seventy miles per hour. But the rugged four-wheel drive truck had an individual character which he relished. It was also an ideal vehicle to use in his woodland.

Entering the rural market town of Petworth, he parked outside the late-night general store in the high street to buy his weekend provisions.

"Good evening, Brenda, I was relying on you still being open."

"Hello Ben, home for the weekend. Nice to see you. I'm sorry to say there are not much fresh vegetables left at this late hour, but we will have everything first thing tomorrow morning."

"That's OK. Bread, ham and a few cans of beer will do me for now."

He paid and continued his journey down the narrow winding street, passing the 17th century Petworth House set behind the high thick outer walls of the seven-hundred-acre deer park, and on towards his house two miles out of town. Petworth is set in the heart of the Sussex Downs National Park. The town is mentioned in Domesday Book as having forty-four households, with twenty-four villagers, eleven smallholders and nine slaves.

Turning off the A283 onto a narrow rural country lane, he drove a short distance before stopping to unlock a five-bar wooden gate. This being the entrance to his home: A detached three-bedroom cottage (built about 1880) and located within twenty acres of woodland. He moved there six years ago with his wife. It had been their dream home. He now lived alone.

People in the village did not know of his previous police employment or of his current role with MI5. From the outset, when asked, he would say he was a freelance legal consultant working in the city and elsewhere. This simple explanation removed the need to identify any company name or location of an office. Enquiries about his occupation were waved away with a light-hearted comment: "A boring job in the city, but it pays the mortgage."

When he worked away from home Mr and Mrs Graysmark, a retired couple living nearby, tended the garden and acted as housekeeper. Both had spent their working lives in the employment of the Petworth House Estate, now owned by the National Trust.

Swan unlocked the front door, entered the hallway and deactivated the alarm. Mrs Graysmark had been in earlier that day and placed the post on the hall table. One letter was marked: 'Confidential. Delivered by hand.'

He sat on a stool in the kitchen to read the letter and flicked on the coffee machine. The letter was brief and signed by the Chief Constable in his distinctive green ink. He had nominated Swan to attend a selection interview for a position with Her Majesty's Inspectorate of Constabulary. The interview was arranged for 3 pm. that coming Monday, in

London. The letter stated Swan should not discuss the matter with anyone. Swan pondered the prospect: *HMI London? Sounds like a boring office secondment, but possibly worthwhile for my CV.*

Swan contemplated on how different life would have been if his wife had not been taken from him. He decided he wanted to spend the weekend alone.

That Friday evening, he poured himself a large whisky and sat reflecting on what had recently happened to him whilst operating in Northern Ireland. Was the letter from his Chief Constable a subtle hint to remove him from his current posting and danger?

Although the 1998 Good Friday Agreement had brought relative peace to Northern Ireland, the threat level from dissident republic paramilitary groups remained at substantial. In recent years, such groups had been responsible for several high-profile bombings and attacks, including the murder of police officers. As a police officer, with the Counter-Terrorism Directorate, he had recently been involved in such an attack.

It had occurred on a dark wet evening when Swan was travelling in an unmarked police car—with a detective inspector from the Police Service of Northern Ireland (PSNI), to a police intelligence conference in West Belfast—and came across a stationery car blocking the road ahead. The vehicle's orange hazard warning lights were flashing, and the bonnet was up. In a quiet calm voice, the DI comment: "Careful, this doesn't feel right."

A shadowy figure, wearing a balaclava and dark clothing, stepped out from behind the bonnet pointing a rifle. There was a loud blast. The windscreen of the police car shattered.

Instinctively, Swan pushed the passenger door open, leaping headfirst onto the grass verge. He rolled into the full prone position with both hands clashing his gun. Six shots were fired in quick succession. The attacker was down. In the darkness there was total silence. No sign of an accomplice.

Swan scrambled to his feet, continued to point his gun at the crumpled figure, and walked towards it. An AK47 semi-automatic rifle remained firmly in the hands of the attacker. He kicked it away a safe distance. He then removed the balaclava and satisfied himself that the man was dead. The contorted face was that of a youth, possibly eighteen or nineteen years of age. What causes such hatred in someone so young: what a useless waste of life.

Turning his attention back to the police car, he saw the shattered windscreen was heavily bloodstained. His colleague had been seriously injured. The DI was conscious, leaning back in much pain, holding his blood-soaked left shoulder. "Fuck me. The transport manager isn't going to be pleased with me for damaging his car." *Police humour in the face of adversity,* thought Swan. The DI survived the attack on his life. Swan was lucky to escape without physical injury.

At the subsequent inquest into the death of the attacker, it was established he had been an active member of a banned paramilitary organisation. Verdict: He had been lawfully killed whilst in the act of attempting to murder police officers. Swan gave evidence from behind a screen, with his identity protected. He was exonerated and commended for his actions.

However, during the hearing, and contrary to policy, it was mentioned that he was not from the PSNI but was an English officer from the UK Counter-Terrorism Directorate. History taught that, during The Troubles, loyalties were often divided and sensitive confidential information sometimes leaked. In time, it was possible his identity would become known to the terrorist organisation and there may be an attempt made to seek revenge.

Swan had been offered the option to be redeployed outside of Ireland but had declined: it was not in his character to run away. For his own protection, he was given special authority to carry a firearm when off duty.

Unanswered and worrying questions remained. On that evening the two officers had been in civilian clothes, driving an unmarked police car to a pre-planned meeting. Information only known by a few people. Yet this was a carefully planned ambush. Clearly there had been an inside leak. Someone working within the police service was willing to assist in the murder of colleagues in cold blood.

Although he had trained, and been an authorised police firearms user for many years, this was the first occasion he had shot someone. He had declined 'counselling', but the circumstances remained very vivid in his mind. The logic was difficult to explain but, following the killing, he felt unable to handle his issued gun and, with the police armourer, had it exchanged for a new gun that had not been fired in anger.

That experience was now in the past. The letter from the Chief Constable gave him the possibility of moving on to another role in his police career.

Before departing for bed, he cleaned and placed his handgun in the safe. It was a Glock 19, the type favoured for off duty and undercover operations. It was smaller and lighter than his previous version and easier to conceal. Also, it had more stopping power than its predecessor and a magazine of 15 rounds. He had made a conscious decision not to wear the gun when in England, whether on or off duty. It would remain in the locked safe.

He rose early on Saturday morning, put on his walking boots and casual clothes, and took a leisurely stroll through his woodland. It was a clear frosty late-February day. The branches on the trees were bare. He walked through the undergrowth, kicking up the fallen rotting leaves and making a mental note of the work he would be undertaking on his next period of leave. He had recently completed a chainsaw course and was keen to test his new-found skill, coppicing the sweet chestnut trees at the far end of his woodland.

Monday morning arrived. Throughout his career Swan had made a point of arriving early for interviews to give him time to relax and prepare. He drove to the local station and caught the fast London bound train to Victoria.

It was a fresh sunny early spring day and, with time to spare, he decided to walk from the station across London to the appointment. The interview was scheduled for 3 pm.

Swan arrived at 2:30 pm. at an austere nondescript government building, with 'bomb proof' net curtains. There was a number, but no name plate on the double doors, which were locked. He pressed the external buzzer, spoke into the intercom to give his details and was allowed entry into the building.

He reported his arrival at the reception desk. As proof of identification, he produced his police warrant card.

On being handed a visitor's badge, he politely enquired for directions to the toilet. The request was declined. He then asked for directions to the canteen and, similarly, it was declined without explanation.

Thirty minutes passed. A woman assistant then escorted him to an oak panelled room, located on the second floor. He was directed to a hard-upright chair, positioned in front of a long wooden desk behind which sat four 'inquisitors'. They did not introduce themselves nor initially appear to acknowledge his presence. He felt unsettled by the prevailing silence. With a degree of annoyance, he thought: *I am not sure I would wish to work with this lot.*

His negative feelings gave him an extra bit of courage.

The chairman opened the conversation by asking if he had had a pleasant journey.

Swan hesitated before responding.

"I apologise for appearing a little ruffled, but I take interviews seriously. My journey here took over two hours and I had calculated to arrive early to gather my thoughts and make myself presentable. Unfortunately, when I arrived at Reception, I was refused access to the gents and to the canteen."

Swan thought: *That's blown it.*

The chairman consulted with the other members and adjourned the interview for five minutes. He directed the woman assistant to escort Swan to the toilet and back.

On retaking his seat, Swan saw a small side table had been positioned next to his chair with a cup of coffee and biscuits. From his previous experience of attending government meetings, he identified, with quiet amusement, the superior chinaware and chocolate biscuits. In Civil Service circles, such luxury was reserved for senior management participation. He smiled and gently nodded towards the chairman: "Many thanks."

The interview continued for over an hour.

Swan was questioned on many aspects of his police career, including operating in Northern Ireland, and on his political and moral attitudes. He did not have a very high opinion of politicians, considering most to be self-serving, arrogant and pompous individuals, but thought it best not to express his personal views. However, he felt at ease with the quality of the questions and with his responses. His instincts picked up on the fact, the interview board did not comment on the proposed role he was seeking within HM Inspectorate.

At the conclusion of the interview, he was asked to wait in a side room. He was aware the selection process was by competition, with several other candidates, and that he was the last to be interviewed. On Swan's return, almost an hour later, the chairman appeared more relaxed and apologised for the slight 'deceit' that had taken place.

"I am the Deputy Director General of the Security Service, more commonly known as MI5. I invite you to join us. Do you wish time to consider?" Very brief and very direct.

Swan felt a little shocked, but more amused.

"I would be honoured to accept. In all honesty, I have little knowledge of your organisation, but it sounds an interesting challenge."

The Deputy Director General smiled.

"That's the way it should be. Once full security clearance has been achieved, you will undergo a training course where everything will become clear. Family, friends and colleagues must not be told of your new role. As far as they are concerned, you will remain a policeman working on some boring project at the Home Office."

Swan was taken to a smaller room. He spent two hours with an officer from the HR department, being briefed and signing numerous documents.

The security checks were completed within the month. His previous police security grading was increased to Enhanced Security Status. He was then called to the London HQ of the Security Service to be advised on his future.

"Welcome to the Security Service. May I be the first to shake your hand" said the Director General. It was Service policy for all new recruits to be welcomed by the top man. Swan was impressed.

Swan spent the rest of the day at further security briefings.

He was given a cover identity.

"We have chosen for you the name Julian Michael Lawson with a new date of birth."

The official handed him a driver's licence, passport and credit cards, all in the new identity,

"From today, you are on the pay-role of the Security Service. However, your role within the Security Service is never publicly acknowledged. We operate under Ministry of Defence (MOD) cover and that is what appears on your ID card."

The official then placed on the table a closed folder marked Secret.

"Your new profile is contained within this file. Please remain here and learn it. Nothing is to be taken from this room. Help yourself to coffee and a colleague will be back in two hours to see you."

Swan opened the file and began reading. He had become a man with a new name and a completely new history.

Everything from name of parents, where born, schools attended, and employment positions were new.

Two hours later, an official entered the room.

"Mr Lawson, I am James from HR, please tell me about yourself."

Swan hesitated for a moment then reiterated the facts he could remember from the profile.

"Very interesting Mr Lawson. What car do you drive?"

Swan looked flustered as he could not recall seeing such details in the profile.

The man continued.

"I know a Graham Lawson who works for Surrey Council, in the pensions department, is he your father?"

Swan stumbled to give a coherent reply and shook his head.

The HR man looked at him showing no emotion.

"It takes time. In all situations, sometimes under intense pressure, your responses must be convincing and accurate. Be back here tomorrow at 9 am to spend a further day on your profile. Colleagues will be here to challenge and assist you. It is an acquired skill not to disclose too much about yourself and to have the confidence to bluff your way through a difficult encounter. Remember, when you get on the train tomorrow you are Julian Lawson and that's the identity which will get you into this building."

Swan leaned forward to speak but was stopped by the man raising the palms of his hands.

"Life does get complicated, but it will soon become second nature. When operating within the arena of the service you are Julian Lawson. However, when at home with friends, neighbours and paying your gas bill, you will continue to be Ben Swan."

"Much like being an actor," replied the new Mr Lawson.

"An actor fluffing his lines might get fired. Fluff your lines and you might get shot – right between the eyes," he said without so much as a smile.

"Leave all the documents here. Good-day, Mr Lawson." He then left the room.

Another unnamed official escorted Swan to a side door and out of the building.

Each day for a week Mr Lawson reported for work at London HQ and the same process continued. He was also briefed on the basic history of the service.

The Security Service (MI5) is the domestic security agency for the United Kingdom. It is responsible for investigating both foreign threats and terrorist activities within the country. Primarily, it is an investigative and surveillance organisation. It has no powers to make arrests.

Its sister organisation is the Secret Intelligence Service (MI6), which operates outside the UK and responsible for foreign intelligence gathering and espionage. It corresponds with the American Central Intelligence Agency (CIA).

MI5 and MI6 initially came into existence as a single organisation, the Secret Service Bureau, in October 1909. The Bureau was formed from Military Intelligence in the lead up to the First World War, to combat fears of German spies operating in the UK and against British interests abroad. The following year, the bureau split into two separate agencies. The new domestic agency operated from room number five in the Military Intelligence department at the Admiralty, hence initials MI5. The foreign agency operated from room number six, hence MI6. The third agency of the UK's national intelligence machinery is the Government Communication Head Quarters (GCHQ) at Cheltenham.

Having mastered his brief, he was handed his new identity documents and a Security Service issued iPhone, which contained additional in-house functions.

Chapter Three

The Training

It was mid-April when Lawson caught the early morning train to London to commence the MI5 month long introductory training course, which ran from Monday to Friday of each week. He still felt uncomfortable using his new identity.

The address was a four-storey Regency building off New Bond Street. The ground floor purported to be a small antiques shop, which always appeared to be closed. In accordance with instructions, he buzzed the intercom at the single side door and spoke his cover name into the intercom.

On the third floor, he was shown into a spacious room furnished with a dozen burgundy coloured leather armchairs positioned in a circle. At the far end, a coffee machine bubbled away on a highly polished table. The window blinds were drawn down restricting natural daylight. The room had the relaxed, but orderly, atmosphere of an army officers' social club.

A woman approached and offered her hand.

"Good morning and welcome. I am Jane, responsible for administration matters. Please help yourself to coffee and fresh croissants."

Jane explained she would not be with the course full-time but would call in most days to check on their well-being.

In a matter of minutes, five other people entered the room and were greeted by Jane. Each smiled and acknowledged other members but did not indulge in a conversation. They sat down in silence, in the comfy chairs, with their coffee and croissants.

Precisely at 9 am, a man entered the room. He was about sixty years of age, slim build and wearing a well cut dark grey pinstripe suit. A distinguished looking individual with short silver-grey hair and rimless spectacles perched on the end of his nose.

"Good morning, I am James the course director." Jane sat down next to him, with her cup of coffee.

Lawson thought: *All these guys seem to be called James*

Together, James and Jane ran through the rules and regulations for the course. This included the fact that no electronic equipment would be brought into the classroom and nothing, including paperwork, would to be removed.

James emphasised on the requirements and responsibilities of the Official Secrets Act 1989.

"The identification of your identity or position by a hostile organisation could prove dangerous to you and the service. It would, undoubtedly, compromise your future career with us.

"You are classified as the Mature Intake. Your average age is thirty-five. All six of you were targeted and selected by the service for your proven ability and identified skills in your previous careers. The Service decided it wanted you. You did not read about us in the Times and send in an application. We will refer to each other by first names only.

"Security Service rules apply from day one: You will not discuss nor disclose each other's background or previous employment."

The new intake consisted of three men and three women.

James explained the course was designed to give a broad overview of the service regarding its functions and departments. The course would receive presentations from senior members of the service and undertake occasional visits to departments. Some evening work would be involved as well. He reiterated the secret nature of the organisation and the reasons why specific details of the departments, staffing and operational issues would not be disclosed.

For the next session, the group adjourned to a conference room on the upper floor, with a single large circular table equipped with a laptop at each position. The tone for the course was professional but informal.

James opened the first presentation.

"Twenty-five years ago, we knew our enemy. The main threat came from the former Soviet Union. Today the world is far more complex. The events of 9/11, and our subsequent involvement in Iraq and Afghanistan, has changed everything. There is now a direct and increasing correlation with espionage and state sponsored terrorism to trigger unstable government.

"To meet the challenges, in ten years, the service has increased significantly: in size, sophistication and technological advancement."

He outlined the UK's position as a major military power and the city of London as the financial capital in the world.

"In addition, this country is a world leader, with our major companies, universities and institutions operating at the forefront of technological, scientific and medical research. All being potential targets.

"In the days of the Cold War, the principal aim was to protect the UK against physical attack from a hostile country. Today, the threat can now come from any of the above, plus from terrorist organisations, groups with a specific agenda and even homegrown individuals.

"Attacks could involve nuclear or conventional explosives, chemical or biological agents and, increasingly, the threat from cyberspace."

Throughout the week presentations and briefings continued.

With the first week of the course concluded, members were free to return home for the weekend. Before departing, James reminded them of their new status and the obligations that went with the role.

"Next week we will be studying surveillance and the technical resources which will be at your disposal. We will also consider the capabilities and activities of foreign hostile agencies, targeted against the UK."

In accordance with policy, the course members left the building separately and Lawson walked across the city to Victoria Railway Station.

Chapter Four
The Mysterious Lady

Back at home in Petworth, in his own environment and with his own identity, he was feeling relaxed. For the weekend, he was now Ben Swan. His MI5 identity documents were securely locked away in the study safe. He did not feel in the mood for cooking, so made himself a cheese bread roll and poured out a whisky. It had been an interesting and, in many respects, a strange week.

He wished his wife had been there to share his experiences. He sat reflecting on their first formal date together: He was then a young detective constable and had invited her to a CID dinner at the Grand Hotel in Brighton. It was an evening-dress affair. Driving to the event, they came across a car crash. The woman driver was seriously injured, lying half out of her car. He immediately stopped his car and rushed to give assistance, gently moving her to the side of the road and out of danger. Unfortunately, she died at the scene. The emergency services quickly arrived and took over. Back in his car, he cleaned the victim's blood from his hands with a wet wipe, and they continued the journey to the function. He never spoke about the incident. Much later in their relationship, his now wife told him that, at the time she had thought he must be a 'hard bastard' not to have been affected by the incident and the death of the woman. However, later she came to understand it was his way of dealing with death: he was actually a caring and sensitive individual.

It was a clear warm Spring Saturday morning and he was sitting in his garden enjoying the smell of early bluebells, drifting across on the gentle breeze from the woods. He folded his copy of the Daily Telegraph and placed it on the garden table. Pouring a second mug of fresh coffee, he pondered on the tasks he had set himself for the day.

His mobile rang. It was his mother asking if she would be seeing him this weekend.

"Hello mum. No, sorry I cannot visit. I have many urgent jobs to do around the house. In fact, I was just off to the farm shop in Billingshurst to buy replacement parts for my chainsaw. I should be home again next Saturday, and I promise to visit you then."

He checked his watch: It was 11:30 am.

Patting his trouser pockets to check he had his car-keys and wallet, he walked through the house, set the alarm, pulled the front door closed and climbed into his Land Rover.

Driving down Shooters Lane he noticed, in the distance, a Land Rover parked on the grass verge. No other vehicles were about in the quiet rural lane. As he approached, he noted the bonnet was up with the driver still seated in the vehicle.

A Land Rover enthusiast would never pass by a fellow Land Rover owner in trouble. He pulled over, parked on the opposite verge and walked towards the truck.

"Can I be of assistance?"

"Thank you. The engine has cut out. Haven't got a clue about mechanical things."

He noted the Land Rover was an early 1970's Series III model in good condition and had been the subject of major restoration. He glanced towards the open bonnet, more interested in the car than the driver.

"Upgraded with a 200 Tdi diesel engine. And it's been nicely done."

The driver's door opened, and a woman climbed out.

"I don't know the history of the car; I've just borrowed it for the day."

Her voice was engagingly seductive. She was slim, in her late twenties, stylishly dressed in an off-white silk casual shirt with designer jeans and brown leather calf-length boots. Her long blonde hair was in a ponytail.

"May I take a look?" He enquired.

The key was still in the ignition. He turned the key several times without a response, then flicked the light switches on and struck the horn with his fist.

"Nothing's working. The battery appears flat or an electrical malfunction."

"I've phoned my uncle and he is bringing a trailer to collect it, but it is going to take about two hours" she said.

"Could I give you a lift somewhere?" He enquired.

She smiled.

"No, I said I'd wait with the car."

She paused in thought.

"But, if it wouldn't be too much of an imposition, is there somewhere nearby where I could get a coffee and something to eat?"

"The local White Hart pub is a couple of miles further on. I would be happy to take you there. It's a former 18th century coaching-house on the old Brighton Road, located by a small river, worth a visit for the view alone."

She smiled and nodded in agreement.

"Yes, please."

He took the keys from the ignition, locked the car and handed them to her.

"Let's go and find that coffee, although, mine might be a beer."

They climbed into the cab of his truck and drove away.

"This is so kind of you. I'm Lucy, what is your name?"

He turned to her and smiled.

"My mum calls me a nuisance."

They arrived at the pub and parked the truck. He directed her towards the garden area and to a wooden table, with bench seats overlooking the river.

"Coffee or beer?"

"Half a pint of lager please"

"Would madam desire a freshly made Ploughman's lunch with a large chunk of Stilton cheese, or a packet of crisps?"

She laughed.

"Hard decision. The Ploughman's please, kind sir."

He went into the pub and returned a few minutes later with the order.

Lucy took her plate.

"This is a beautiful part of the world. I wouldn't mind settling down around here."

"Not a local girl then?"

"No, my family home is in West Yorkshire. I attended a private boarding school in Cambridge and then after university, travelled the world stopping off for a couple of years in Australia and then America."

"Sounds exciting."

"It has been, but now it's time to settle down and do other things."

"So how come you end up by the side of the road with a broken-down Land Rover?"

She took a slip of her lager.

"I arrived back in the UK last week and have been staying with my aunt and uncle on their farm in Hampshire, whilst I take time-out to consider my future. This morning, my uncle suggested I borrow the Land Rover to adventure out into the countryside. How about you?"

He sat back with the glass of beer in his hand.

"Boring job in the city, but it pays sufficiently well to allow me my passion for living in the countryside."

They laughed and chatted about how she was hopeless at map reading and had not realised she had strayed into Sussex.

"Forty-year-old Land Rovers don't come equipped with Satnav."

He found Lucy attractive and could image her in his house being the perfect host at an informal dinner party: Just like the old days.

Lucy interrupted his thoughts.

"Is there a Mrs Nuisance?"

The happiness visibly drained from his face.

"There was once."

Lucy appeared upset.

"Sorry, I didn't mean to pry. Excuse me, I must visit the lady's room."

Ben watched, as she walked away across the garden talking on her mobile. He liked her very much.

On her return, Ben smiled at Lucy.

"It's me who should say sorry. Some things still feel a little raw."

She relaxed and stretched out her arms.

"This is lovely: The location, the food and the company. The day was going badly, then along came my knight in shining armour and rescued me."

"Well in an old shiny Land Rover actually. But at least it's one that works."

She laughed and moved closer to him. Hugging his arm, she kissed him on the right cheek.

"Thank you, Mr Nuisance."

A tingle ran down the back of his neck. She possessed a happy personality and was fun to be with.

Lucy held his left hand and turned it towards her to check the time on his watch.

"A Mont Blanc Timewalker. Very discrete and understated, a good quality in a man."

She looked up at him and smiled.

"I've just spoken with my uncle. He should be arriving at the Land Rover within hour. If you can drop me back there, I'll wait for him."

When they finished their lunch, Ben drove slowly back and parked his truck behind the Series III.

"Would you like me to wait with you?"

"No, that will not be necessary. I have a good book to keep me company."

She leaned across towards him.

"Shall I leave you my mobile number? Perhaps as a proper thank you, I could take you out for a meal one evening?"

He responded in a quiet caring voice.

"Thank you, but not at the moment I have a lot going on,"

She accepted the gentle rebuff.

He noticed Lucy had a small piece of paper in her hand which, on his rejection, she discreetly slipped into the side pocket of her jeans. It was probably her telephone number, which she had intended to give.

Lucy gave him a kiss on his cheek.

"It would be nice to see you again. You are a gentleman."

She jumped down from the cab of his Land Rover and ran to her vehicle.

As he drove away, he looked in his rear-view mirror to see her waving good-bye. In a quiet voice he commented to himself.

"Lucy, you are something special and I like the fragrance of your perfume."

It had been over a year since his wife died. This was the first time he had felt an emotional attachment to another woman. He thought her to be attractive with a genuine and fun personality.

Chapter Five

Revealing the Truth

The second week of the MI5 course resumed at 9 am. on Monday morning. The group assembled in the conference room on the third floor of the training complex. All six recruits were present and quickly took their seats. Jane entered the room and served fresh coffee and croissants. James then entered in company with another man who he introduced as Patrick to talk on the service's surveillance and operational capabilities. No further introduction or identification was given: this was normal practice when introducing visiting speakers

Patrick was a man in his mid-forties, smartly dressed in a well-cut dark suit with the military bearing of someone in authority. He remained standing and opened his presentation without the slightest hint of a smile. The man appeared devoid of humour.

"At the outset, I offer no apology for not discussing the size of my department. Nor will I give detailed technical information on how we conduct such operations. It is enough to say: the department is well resourced and has a proven track record second to none.

"I will give you an example of our work and what service you can expect. When you become an operational agent, report to us what you are seeking to achieve. My department will draw up the operational specification, execute the plan and deliver to you the result."

He walked across to a large wall mounted screen.

"The essence of a successful operation is that the target is unaware he or she is under surveillance.

"However, there are occasions when we deliberately engage with the unsuspecting target for the purpose of gaining intelligence. In such cases there are five elements to the operation:

- HQ Base Control
- Forward Control
- The Technical Team
- The Watchers. The team that undertakes the physical surveillance and
- The Instigator. This individual engages with the target.

The following is a recent exercise we undertook. I will comment on the basic techniques deployed."

He tapped the keypad of his laptop and on the large screen, appeared a Google map image of the world.

He tapped again. It zoomed in on a photographic image of the UK.

"This is a location in Southern England. The image was obtained using a military satellite, a much higher resolution that of a commercial satellite. Let me illustrate."

He tapped the keypad and gave a wry smile.

The image rapidly zoomed in to display, on the screen, the front page of a newspaper.

"From one hundred and eighty miles up in space, we can read the lead story in last Saturday's Daily Telegraph."

He moved to the centre of the room to face his audience.

"In fact, Julian, it is your newspaper."

Lawson focused on the screen with a sense of bewilderment. He did not move nor comment.

Patrick returned to his previous position.

"The exercise was undertaken, primarily, to show this course and what is available to you. Plus, to demonstrate the potential dangers of being targeted by a hostile agency. Also, it was a valuable training opportunity for my staff."

Lawson looked at Patrick. There was confusion and anger in his voice. He had taken an instant disliking of the man.

"So, when I was in my garden, you took photographs of me having breakfast?"

Sensing Lawson's annoyance, Patrick slowly walked towards him.

"The operation involved much more than that."

"How much more?"

"Everything."

Lawson shook his head and frowned.

"Sorry, I don't understand. What do you mean: Everything?"

Standing in front of him, Patrick leaned slightly forward.

"The broken-down Land Rover. A Series III I believe."

Lawson stood up as if to challenge Patrick at the same eye level.

"It was a setup then!"

He remained silent for several seconds before continuing with the challenge.

"How did you know I was going to be travelling down that lane?"

Patrick raised his right hand, to defuse the situation, and gently gestured Lawson to sit down.

"You told your mother when and where you were going."

"So, my mobile was being monitored?"

"Yes."

Lawson felt even more confused and angry, as the full position became evident.

"And the girl was part of it?"

"Yes. She is a very skilled member of my team."

Patrick tapped his laptop and, on the screen, appeared a series of ground and satellite photographs of the events of Saturday morning.

"Homework for such an operation includes knowing what makes the target tick. We identified your passion for Land Rovers and the unwritten ethos that an enthusiast will always stop to help another. Especially when a tempting Series Three is dangled as bait."

Looking at the photographs Lawson's level of anger remained high.

"What was the logic in going to the pub?"

Patrick stepped back.

"The object of the exercise was to obtain as much information as possible from the target i.e. you. In a real-life situation, we would endeavour to compromise the target and develop it to the next stage."

Possibly wary of Lawson's next response, he took another step back.

"I must say, Mr Nuisance, you didn't give much away. Not even your name. Well played."

Lawson was not enjoying the game. Internally his emotions were in turmoil – with elements of embarrassment.

Patrick stayed his distance.

"Once in your car, you told Lucy the name and location of the pub which allowed us to deploy the Watchers, who were in place when you arrived."

Lawson tapped his knuckles together.

"So, you observed us having lunch?"

Patrick remained standing in the same position.

"As this was an exercise, for testing staff and equipment, we also deployed a small drone which, in effect, is a sophisticated and almost silent radio-controlled plane.

"You will recall Lucy held your wrist and turned it to check the time of your watch."

A photograph of the face of Lawson's watch appeared on the screen.

"This was taken using the drone. The clarity is impressive. We can even read the date."

Feeling a little more confident that Lawson was beginning to appreciate the logic for the exercise, Patrick moved closer to the group.

"So, a successful operation. It has shown what we are about and what we can offer you. Also, my staff and I found it to be a useful training exercise."

Lawson thought to himself: *Bastard.*

At the lunch break, he was still feeling angry so he walked across to St. James Park and sat on a bench under the shade of a willow tree. For several minutes, he sat in silence gazing out on the park.

"Hello, Mr Nuisance."

He looked up and saw 'Lucy' standing to his right looking guilty and self-conscious. She was dressed in a smart business style grey jacket and skirt with her long blonde hair flowing off her shoulders. For an instant he felt pleased to see her, but then remembered the morning's surveillance presentation.

"Julian, may I sit down. It would be wrong to apologise for doing my job but, on a personal note, may I say sorry."

She sat down next to him.

He looked annoyed.

"How did you know I was here? Still tracking me with your silly radio-controlled toy in the sky."

"Please don't be cynical. I was due to be with Patrick at the presentation but decided to stay out of the way. I sensed you would be upset. I saw you leave the building and I wanted to explain."

"Now it's my time to ask, what do I call you?"

"Possibly you are thinking Miss Nasty. My mum says I am a nice person. The name is Sally. Sally Chambers. Can we be friends?"

He gave a conciliatory smile.

"Regulations states that a relationship between staff must be reported to HR. Probably in triplicate."

She laughed.

"We haven't even held hands yet, it's a long way from a relationship. How about taking me up on my earlier offer of a meal? Colleagues are permitted to dine with fellow officers."

Lawson turned towards her and playfully stroked his chin as if contemplating his reply.

She gently prodded him.

"I know you like me. You even like the fragrance of my perfume."

"Explain yourself Miss Nasty."

"Sorry, I left a bug in your car. It was part of the exercise. I heard what you said when you drove off. All bugs have now been removed, exercise over."

Lawson's anger was again visible.

"Sally or whatever your name is. Do you know my true background?"

"Partly. In confidence, to prepare for the sting exercise, I was made aware of your home address and that you were recruited from the police. But that is about it: only given information we need to know."

Lawson bit his lip and took a deep intake of air.

"In my previous career, I dealt with many murders, went to countless post-mortems and worked on terrorist bombings."

He stopped in mid-sentence to compose himself.

"But none made me feel as uneasy as I felt this morning at the presentation."

He took a further deep breath.

"On a professional level I was impressed with the operation. On an emotional level, it really hurt."

Sally leaned towards him.

"Professionally I was pleased with my performance. I must separate the work me from the real caring me. You will have experienced the same when dealing with the bad guys."

There was a moment of silence between them before he showed a trace of a smile.

"OK, all is forgiven."

"So how about that meal?" she retorted.

Lawson shook his head.

"A confession: I have a loathing for noisy London restaurants. I always seem to end up sitting near an irritating woman with specs on top of her head, talking loudly into her mobile."

She smiled.

"So, also a grumpy person."

He laughed.

"It's my age."

"When I said good-bye to you last Saturday, I said you were a gentleman and hoped we would meet again. That was the caring me talking."

Lawson laughed.

"Mr Nuisance and Miss. Nasty announce their friendship. That has a certain ring to it."

The couple walked back to New Bond Street and went their different ways.

As he reached the top of the stairs to the training complex he was met by Jane.

"Julian, I just wanted to have a word."

She guided him to the coffee machine and poured out a mug of coffee which she handed to him, "Sally said she was going to have a chat with you. I trust you parted friends?"

Lawson nodded.

"Yes, we did. I now understand the reason for the exercise, and I've learned a valuable lesson."

He shrugged his shoulders.

"It's a hard world."

Jane put her hand on his shoulder.

"Dangerous too. In this game people are rarely what they purport to be."

She showed understanding.

"I'm here to sort out admin issues but, don't forget, I'm also here for personal matters. The service is a close-knit family and we protect each other."

Jane was a woman in her mid-forties with an air of quiet dignity. She dressed in keeping with that of a businesswoman in the city and wore her glasses on a slim gold chain around her neck. She was probably a manager in HR.

Four weeks passed quickly. Days consisted of presentations by speakers from the service, government and other agencies. Most were only identified by their first name. In respect of MI5 personal, the nature of their department and how they functioned remained obscure. The maxim was: Cannot say too much, just tell us what you want, and we will deliver.

The two representatives from MI6 were the most secretive. Following their departure, one of the group joked:

"It was a shame MI6 didn't turn up, but James showed initiative by going out in the street and finding two strangers to come in to talk about nothing."

Lawson found the presentations on cryptography, the science of information security, and code breaking fascinating but somewhat confusing. Long before they spoke on the laws of quantum physics, he had lost the plot.

He acknowledged to himself that cryptanalysts and computer scientists operated in a world he did not understand. There was clearly much going on in the world of communication, interception of which most people were not aware.

On occasions, the group was also taken in people carriers with darken windows, to various government establishments for practical demonstrations on equipment, communications and control facilities. The exact locations were not disclosed.

There was no 'end of course party', no group photograph or exchange of telephone numbers. No one promised to meet again. Each was assigned to their designated section to disappear into the large secret void that is the British Security Service.

Strangely, although they did not know each other's true identity, a deep bond of trust and commitment had developed between the course members. Each possessed a distinctive and strong character. Throughout, professionalism and humour had been present in abundance.

Before departing, each member had a final briefing with Jane.

"Julian, how did you find the course?"

He paused for a moment to reflect before answering.

"It's a strange feeling. I've learned a lot but feel I know little."

She nodded as if understanding his predicament.

"Please explain."

He folded his arms and pulled a face in puzzlement.

"I have a clear picture of the role and function of the service. I know what is expected from me. I know what the various departments can do but, and it is a big but, the 'whole' remains a mystery."

He gesticulated with the palms of his hands open.

"Who are the people I am working with? How are results achieved? What is a result? It is like going to a magic show. You watch the tricks being performed but, you come away not knowing how."

"An interesting analogy. Please continue."

He unfolded his arms and rested them on the sides of the chair.

"Over the last couple of weeks, I have been reading Christopher Andrew's book on the service titled: The Defence of the Realm. It is nearly a thousand pages long. When I finished, my thoughts were rather ambivalent.

"Somehow, I knew a lot but, at the same time, had gained nothing tangible about the service. That is how I feel about the course. Is that normal?"

Jane smiled.

"Exactly. Remember this is a secret organisation. It is designed and functions in a group of tightly controlled spheres, which are reliant, but independent of each other. If one part is damaged, the rest of the organisation is not compromised. I believe you will fit in well. May I wish you all the best?"

Chapter Six

Operation Brimstone

Thames House, London Headquarters of MI5, is in Mill Bank on the north side of River Thames. An imposing Grade II listed building, purchased by the government in 1988 and, after extensive refurbishment, opened as the HQ for MI5 in 1994. The considerable physical and electronic defences are not immediately apparent.

The main entrance in Mill Bank is used by visitors who attend by appointment, which explains the lack of external door handles. The façade is the public perception of the Security Service often pictured in the media.

Staff enters via one of the several doors located along the rear of the building accessed from a side street. The road is under twenty-four hours a day camera surveillance and monitored by security guards. Any person or vehicle found loitering is moved on. A small indicator is located at either end of the road, positioned so that strangers are not aware of its significance, and activated when it is suspected the building is under surveillance by a hostile agency i.e. the Media or other groups, interested in photographing MI5 staff. When such a warning is in place staff will walk on and not enter the building until the all-clear sign is given.

Prior to 1990, the government did not publicly acknowledge the existence of its security services. In recent years, MI5 has slightly come out of the shadows. The location of its HQ and function is now in the public arena, and the name of the Director General is known. However, the identities of operational members of the service remain strictly guided. When required to give evidence at a court of law, or before a government committee, agents will give it from behind a screen and without disclosing their identity.

The Headquarters of its sister organisation, the Secret Intelligence Service, better known to the public as MI6, is located further along the River Thames at Vauxhall Cross. The futuristic designed building is the one portrayed in the James Bond films.

It was 8:15 am on Monday morning when Lawson arrived for work at Thames House. Two months had passed since he began operational duties. His office was situated on the second floor. Apart from the number, there was no other sign on the door to indicate his office. This policy applies to all offices within the building.

Using his security ID swipe card, he unlocked the door, entered, and closed it behind him. As he sat down, his thoughts were on the previous day, Sunday, when he had attended the interrogation suite in Admiralty Arch to interview Barry Marsh on behalf of the Foreign Office: i.e. the staff driver who, in Moscow, had been the target of a 'honeytrap' sting. He pondered on the various tasks he had undertaken in the two months since his arrival. It had covered a large spectrum of activity and had involved using the facilities of various sections and liaising with different security agencies – at home and abroad. He was beginning to feel an integral part of the service.

On the desk in front of him sat a computer and a telephone but nothing else. Departmental policy dictated that whenever the office was vacated all files and other material must be placed in the locked office safe. No family photographs or items, which might identify the occupant, were permitted to be displayed. Security was paramount in respect of documents and the identity of agents.

Lawson sat at his desk thinking about his current existence and comparing it with his life as a police officer. As a newly promoted detective chief inspector at a new station, he had walked the corridors to visit offices and introduced himself to the staff, to gain an understanding of their roles. The environment within the service was totally different.

Corridors on each floor were identical, with closed and locked doors on either side. There was no signage, just a number on a door. Each department was within a separate secure area, accessible only by those with the approved security clearance electronically registered on their ID card.

Staff only visited another office or section by appointment. A casual walk around the building for an informal chat with a colleague was not only prohibited but also impossible. He missed the camaraderie of the police service. Most police stations had a social club where officers could relax, away from public scrutiny, in the company of colleagues who shared and understood the often unpleasant and dangerous elements of the job.

Lawson logged into the desktop computer to check his electronic diary: '09:00 to 12:00 hrs. Silver Conference Room. Briefing.' It gave no further explanation. He looked at his watch: it was eight-fifty-five. The conference room was on the top floor. He immediately logged off, locking the door behind him, and quickly made his way to the briefing.

The six conference rooms situated on the top floor are identified by colour – Gold, Silver and Bronze etc. Silver is the second largest. For security reasons, the rooms do not have external windows and before each meeting they are electronically swept for bugging devices.

Lawson entered the conference room a couple of minutes before nine. He was surprised to see familiar faces. Standing at one end of the room, drinking coffee, were the other five members from the training course.

"What's this, I didn't think we had course reunions?" he said with a broad grin of pleasure.

Jane Rigby stepped into his line of sight.

"Yes, like old times. Please help yourself to coffee. This is going to be a three-hour session."

He turned towards her.

"Jane, it's good to see you. So, they have roped you in again to keep an eye on us and serve coffee."

She smiled and called out, "Please take your seats. We have much to go through."

The seven took their seats at the round conference table. Each position was equipped with a laptop computer. A large wall mounted screen flickered into life.

Clasping both hands around her coffee mug, Jane leaned forward and looked round the table at each team member.

"It is two months since the end of the course. Individually, your progress has been carefully monitored. It gives me satisfaction to report that the service is pleased with what you have achieved and with your professionalism and integrity. We can now move forward."

She stood up, putting on her spectacles.

"I am Director of Special Operations and, as from now, you are part of my team."

Lawson slowly sat back in his chair raising his eyebrows.

Jane observed his reaction and smiled.

"Julian, I did warn you that in this game people are rarely what they purport to be."

He nodded to her in agreement. He had thought her a rather motherly support member from Human Resources. Now she had disclosed she was a director – only one rank below the Deputy Director General. In his mind she grew in stature.

On the large screen appeared the words 'Operation Brimstone'.

Jane walked to the wall screen.

"The threat from terrorism is increasing. It is not going away. The complexity of terrorist operations is increasing. Six months ago, the service decided additional staff—with certain skills and talents—was required to meet the challenges and we came hunting. From the outset, you were selected and recruited to be part of Special Operations. Welcome to the team. There is much work to do."

She continued, "We have a new major terrorist threat. It could be the 'big one' long predicted by experts. Intelligence from a trusted source indicates that many millions of dollars have been made available to fund the attack. The source of the funding is currently not known. The intention is for a major and sustained terrorist attack against the UK mainland. The threat is considered credible."

Lawson asked, "Is there any suggestion who is supplying the money."

Jane replied, "The amount involved would suggest a wealthy backer. It could be an individual or, more likely, a rouge state. However, at this early stage, nothing can be ruled in and nothing must be ruled out."

Helen, a member of the group queried, "Is that not a great deal of money to suggest a donation from one individual?"

Jane, responded, "There are unscrupulous multi-billionaires in many parts of the world who would regard such a sum as pocket money."

Another member quipped, "Russian oligarchs in this country pay more than that for a Premier Division footballer or a piece of art."

Jane stood by the large screen.

"The current threat level from inter-national terrorism in the UK is assessed as SEVERE. This means a terrorist attack is highly likely. In recent years, we have thwarted eighteen potential attacks. Several resulted in criminal court convictions with long terms of imprisonment." She paused and added in a quieter voice, "However, many were neutralised without the public being made aware."

Photographs were flashed on screen of the nine-eleven attacks in America and the seven-seven attacks in London.

"The multiple attacks in New York and London were carried out by suicide bombers during a single day. In the case of America, their chosen weapons were aircraft. And in the London attacks: conventional homemade explosives."

Jane walked back to her position at the conference table, picked up a folder and returned to the screen.

"Intelligence indicates the money has been placed at the disposal of Al Qaeda. Analysis of intercepted communications gives cause to believe the group may be receiving advice from military sources and IT experts—this strengthens the possibility of involvement with a rouge state."

She paused and removed her spectacles.

"The terrorists aim to pull-off a 'spectacular' by multiple attacks, possibly over a period of days, on nationally important elements of this country's infrastructure. In short, to cause severe disruption, destruction and loss of life. This would result in long-term damage to the economic well-being of this country."

Paul Westbrook raised his hand.

"Jane, why the UK and not the US?"

Jane answered, "Firstly, may I address you as a group. The Service has reached a position where we have full trust and confidence in your integrity, which enables us to slightly relax the rules. I can disclose Paul was an army major with Special Forces. We will discuss your respective talents later."

She then continued, "Now to answer Paul's question. America is Al Qaeda's number one target with the UK being number two. However, an attack on the UK requires fewer resources to achieve the same goal. We are a small crowded island, heavily reliant on the import and export of goods by air and sea, and everything radiates or is controlled from the centre—i.e. London. A devastating attack on our supply lines and or the centre, would paralyse the economic well-being of the entire country. In comparison, America is vast. Gaining access into America presents greater logistical problems and hitting one centre, i.e. New York or Washington, would have less comparative effect on the rest of the country."

The meeting discussed how previous terrorist attacks had been carried out in London. To combat attacks from the IRA, the 'ring of steel' had been established around the city with checkpoints, a significant increase in policing activity, extensive CCTV coverage and other sophisticated systems: which severely limited the terrorist's ability to drive car bombs into the city. The IRA objective was to plant an explosive device and escape to safety before it detonated. The events of nine-eleven and seven-seven changed all that. The terrorists were now likely to be suicide bombers intending to die in the explosion.

A member of the team queried, "What evidence is there to suggest Al Qaeda involvement?"

Jane replied, "Voice analysis had identified two Individuals. One is an Al Qaeda operative currently on the FBI's 'Ten Most Wanted Terrorists' list. He has been implicated in a series of bombing attacks in East Africa in nineteen ninety-eight. There has been no reliable sighting of him for about ten years. The second individual has been matched by voice analysis with telephone calls, monitored eleven years earlier in respect of the attack on the USS Cole. He was never identified."

Jane explained, the intercepted mobile telephone traffic into the UK had originated from East Africa, Pakistan and Yemen. The suggestion was that 'the centre' for planning was in Pakistan where decisions on targets would be made. Calls had been made and received on 'pay-as-you-go' mobile telephones.

Email traffic had also been intercepted between an unknown individual using an internet café in Manchester, with an unknown user at an internet café in Yemen. Messages had been in code with action taken to evade identification of the people involved.

Jane continued, "They appear to be accessing the practicability of deploying not only explosives, but also biological, chemical or radioactive weaponry. Intercepted voice communications indicate internet attacks on major institutions are also being considered."

Paul asked, "And where are the suggested targets?"

Jane replied, "They intend it to be a 'spectacular'. Suggested targets include London's financial centre, the national transport system, air and seaports; and national gas and electric utilities. We do not possess a definitive script of their intended targets or weapons or timescale. That is the challenge."

The meeting adjourned for coffee and a comfort break.

Lawson walked over to the coffee machine and, with a mischievous smile, spoke with Jane.

"Tell me this is for real and not another training exercise."

She handed him a coffee.

"It's for real. The complexity and daring of terrorist attacks has been increasing. It was inevitable they would eventually go for the really big one."

The meeting resumed. They were joined by an analyst from the service's Joint Terrorism Analysis Centre.

She commenced, "Currently, the intelligence is slim on specifics, but it is a dangerous situation. We could be at the beginning of a long-haul. However, there are worrying indications it could be soon."

The analyst projected various charts onto the screen and discussed the case of the nine-eleven attacks in America, "Eighteen suicide bombers seized and crashed five aircraft on that day. We estimate the time from initial planning to execution took two years."

Jane interjected, "The case presented to you this morning is far more complex. However, at the present time, we do not have enough intelligence to accurately gauge how far they have advanced the plan. However, the scale of their ambitions can be to our advantage. The more people involved, the greater the opportunity for us to intercept their communications and identify them and their base locations."

The analyst continued, "Let me give a brief overview on some of the Al Qaeda attacks against the US:

"The 'US Embassy Bombings' refer to a series of attacks that occurred on seventh August nineteen-ninety-eight in Nairobi, Kenya and Dar-es-Salaam in Tanzania. Two hundred and fifty-eight people died and more than five thousand were injured.

"On October 2, 2000, there was a water-borne suicide attack against the United States Navy destroyer USS Cole, while anchored in the Yemeni harbour of Aden. Seventeen sailors were killed."

Paul commented, "Regarding the embassy attacks. The US launched cruise missiles later that month, striking a terrorist training complex in Afghanistan and destroying a pharmaceutical manufacturing facility in Khartoum, Sudan that was producing nerve gas."

The analyst added, "And this is a good example of an individual funding terrorism. Both establishments were financed by Osama bin Laden. He was born in Saudi Arabia— his father was a billionaire. Bin Laden was reputed to have had a personal fortune of over two hundred and fifty million dollars."

He continued, "You will be aware that US Special Forces and CIA operatives shot and killed him in Abbottabad, Pakistan. Following his death, there was understandable concern that Al Qaeda may seek retaliation. We have a small team working in America with the CIA and FBI, analysing material seized during the raid. It is of interest to us that the intercepted traffic indicated a 'spectacular' against the UK began a week after the death of bin Laden."

Jane added, "It is possible that the planning for an attack on the UK has been in being for up to two years, and is well advanced, but we just haven't picked up the intelligence. May I repeat my earlier words of caution – 'nothing should be ruled in and nothing must be ruled out.' GCHQ is currently involved in a large-scale trawling operation and we expect an update, and possible breakthrough, within two days. We must be prepared to move quickly and from now, the team will acquire immediate response status. The Director General is aware of the situation and has briefed the Government's Joint Intelligence Committee on Operation Brimstone."

Chapter Seven

Judgement Day

06:00 hours: MS Spirit of Britain, sailing from Calais, was the first cross-channel ferry of the day to berth at the Port of Dover. The large bow doors opened, disgorging dozens of lorries and cars down the metal ramp and onto the dockside Hundreds of foot passengers followed, primarily young holidaymakers returning to or arriving in the UK, having taken the overnight crossing to save on hotel accommodation.

The young slim man dressed in a dark blue loose-fitting ski jacket, with the hood up and carrying a backpack, blended in with other passengers. The small European Union flag attached to the side of his backpack and the England tourist guide in his hand suggested he was a foreign visitor to the UK. He approached customs and ambled confidently through the 'Nothing to Declare' channel and on into the nearby Costa Coffee restaurant.

He purchased a coffee and sat alone at a table facing the main glass door. His hood remained covering his head. He was deliberately avoiding eye contact or communication with other diners. After fifteen minutes, he left the restaurant and headed to the departure terminal where he purchased a one-way bus ticket to London and boarded the awaiting National

Express coach. He slowly walked up the aisle of the coach taking a seat near the rear. He placed his backpack on the seat next to him to discourage being joined by another passenger. The eighty-mile journey would take approximately two hours.

A silent figure moved into the vacant restaurant seat. He discreetly picked up the empty cardboard coffee cup, discarded by the young male traveller, and placed it into an exhibit bag, which he sealed and placed in his jacket pocket: The Security Service had secured the DNA and fingerprints of the unidentified man. Other members of the surveillance team had also been covertly photographing the suspect.

GCHQ had been tracking him—via his mobile telephone signal—since he left Yemen two weeks earlier. The mobile had been used to communicate with a terrorist cell in Manchester, but the identity of the user remained unknown. During the sea crossing he had been under physical surveillance and, as the ferry approached mid-channel, he was observed to throw his mobile phone into the sea. The phone had served its purpose and he was now ensuring any incriminating evidence it contained would sink with it to the bottom of the English Channel.

The target sat in the rear section of the London bound coach. As the coach left the port, he was observed wearing stereo headphones and clearly not intending to engage in conversation with other passengers. En-route, the coach was under observation from a following unmarked Special Branch car.

Arriving at Victoria Station Coach Terminal and before alighting he put on a woollen beanie hat, pulling it tightly down over his forehead. He walked around the shopping complex and into the street, occasionally looking into shop windows viewing the reflection to check if he was being followed. The confident and knowledgeable way he walked around indicated he was familiar with the area and had received training in counter-surveillance techniques. This gave his Watchers added confidence they had the 'right man' in their sights.

Satisfied he was not under surveillance; he entered the Victoria train station and approached the locker bay. As an extra precaution, he then remained still for a minute or more to check that he was not being watched. Taking a key from his pocket, he opened locker number fifty-six and retrieved a new pay-as-you-go mobile phone and a single second-class train ticket to Manchester.

He switched on the mobile phone and placed it in his jacket top pocket. As he stood on the concourse viewing the electronic departure board, his mobile phone rang. He answered it and held a brief conversation with the caller. Checking the time on his wristwatch, he then proceeded to board the intercity train to Manchester.

The carefree looking young woman standing nearby, holding her boyfriend's hand, checked the incoming text message on her mobile: 'TARGET HAS MADE CONTACT WITH MANCHESTER. CONFIRMED HE IS OUR MAN. OPERATION BROMSTONE IS ACTIVATED.' She smiled and showed the text message to her 'boyfriend'. The couple boarded the Manchester-bound train. The time was 09:30 hours.

For several days the surveillance team, which included Lawson, Paul Westbrook and his colleagues, had been on standby at their London base for immediate deployment. The surveillance team comprised of six high-powered cars, with three persons in each, and three motorcyclists riding BMW R1200 GS sports bikes. The team would operate as three groups, with two cars and a motorcycle in each. Each of the three groups was allocated a call sign: Bluebird Zero One, Bluebird Zero Two and Bluebird Zero Three. Each vehicle was specially equipped for long range surveillance and tracking equipment, with direct communication links with Central Command.

In addition, a Mercedes van provided the support to the team. With a crew of four, it was equipped with sophisticated satellite communications and the latest technology in photographic and thermal imaging equipment. It also carried a small military radio-controlled drone, capable of relaying back live video.

Jane Rigby, the department's director, would take on the role of the team's Field Operations Manager and operate from the Mercedes support vehicle, with the call sign "Motherbird."

At 09:35 hours the team received a text message: 'OP BRIMSTONE. IMMEDIATE. REPORT TO OFFICERS' MESS RAF BRIZE NORTON. SECURITY GATE AWARE.'

RAF Brize Norton is in Oxfordshire, sixty-five miles northwest of London. It is the largest military airbase in the UK and home of Strategic and Tactical Air transport. The team arrived at the security gate and on production of their MOD identification were, without questions or searches, directed to the Officers' Mess.

Jane briefed the team: recent reliable intelligence had established that four of the Manchester cell were about to undertake a journey by car to Scotland. Their destination was a remote holiday lodge located in the hills above Loch Linnhe, at the foot of the Glencoe mountain range. It was located about fifteen miles from the town of Fort William and ten miles from the nearest inhabited property. The lodged had been booked for just a three-day stay from a travel agency in London. Enquiries had established payment had been by cash and a false name and address had been given.

The 'target' from the morning ferry, which for the duration of the operation had been designated the code name Spitfire, was meeting up in Manchester with two other members of the cell. They would then travel by car to meet up with the other four at the lodge. It was intended as a planning and training weekend. Intelligence states they will, during their stay in Scotland, take delivery of weapons and explosives. Of additional concern was an indication that the package would include radioactive material.

She added, "As we speak, a covert entry operation is underway at the lodge to install listening and recording equipment. We will need to be in position and fully operational by the time they cross the border to Scotland. By road, it is a five hundred miles plus journey. So, courtesy of the RAF, in ten minute we will be loaded onto a Lockheed C-130J Hercules military-transport aircraft and flown to RAF Machinist. Flying at three hundred miles per hour, we will be there and landed within the next two hours."

Jane handed each section of the team a detailed briefing document to be read whilst in flight. "The aim of the operation is to closely monitor and record the cell's activities and obtain a profile and photograph of each member. We will be operating under the direction and control of Central Command."

The giant four-engine turboprop C130J Hercules was quickly loaded with the vehicles and personnel. A second smaller aircraft was also deployed for the operation. On this, was loaded a long wheelbase four-by-four Land Rover Defender. It was kitted out to resemble a mountain rescue vehicle and came with six men dressed in appropriate clothing. They wore balaclavas and from the outset, did not mix with the other members of the team. Jane simply acknowledged them as, "Special Forces to provide additional support."

14:00 hours: The two aircraft landed at RAF Machrihanish and, with the minimum of ceremony, discharged their human and vehicular cargo. The military ground crew had been briefed to expect the arrival of the two aircrafts and were aware of the need for secrecy. The formal paper documentation relating to landing authorisation was exchanged without either party entering into detailed conversation beyond the necessary acknowledgments.

The air station is situated on the western side of the Kintyre peninsula. Its remoteness and isolation make it an ideal location for such a sensitive operation. During the Cold War, it was a NATO facility managed by the US military and used to accommodate a unit of their Navy Seals. It is now maintained by the MOD for training exercises and held in readiness in times of conflict or natural emergency.

By late afternoon, the respective surveillance groups— Bluebird Zero One and Bluebird Zero Two—were deployed and had picked up the two target cars travelling independently up the A82 main road and into the Highlands. The targets were also being tracked by satellite surveillance. Bluebird Zero Three was already in position, parked on a quiet mountain track, undertaking long range surveillance on the lodge and the surrounding area. By nightfall, the terrorists were all together in the lodge and settled down for the night. They had a busy schedule planned for the following day.

06:15 hours: A seagoing motor-sailing yacht, monitored cruising in the Atlantic Ocean along the west coast of Scotland, entered the Sound of Mull and under engine power, continued into Loch Linnhe. It was not unusual to see holiday boats sailing in the loch heading to the small port at Fort William at the north east end. However, in this case GCHQ had, during the night, picked up mobile phone contact with individuals on the yacht and a mobile phone in the lodge. The text sent from the yacht was simple but confirmed association: 'EXPECT PACKAGE WITHIN THE HOUR.'

06:55 hours: The yacht cut engine power and dropped anchor two hundred metres from the deserted and wooded shoreline. There were two men onboard. One climbed into an inflatable dingy and headed to the shore. As it approached, two men stepped out from the treeline steadying the bow of the craft as it beached. Only brief words of acknowledgement were exchanged, before a large holdall was quickly handed to the two men on the shore. The craft was swiftly turned around and motored back to the yacht, which then immediately weighed anchor and headed back out to sea. Central Command directed no intervention of the fleeing yacht by the team. It would remain under satellite surveillance: the fate of the crew having been decided.

The holdall was carried the short distance back to the lodge to be greeted enthusiastically by the other men.

07:30 hours. The cell of seven men left the lodge and headed on foot towards the uninhabited Glencoe valley, each carrying a heavy backpack and wearing clothing commensurate with that of regular hill walkers. All wore balaclavas making personal identification difficult. Under constant covert surveillance, the group walked for about two miles and, before coming to a stop, carefully looked around to ensure no one else was in the neighbourhood.

Satisfied that they were alone in the valley, they unstrapped their backpacks and placed them on the ground. From each a package was taken out and opened revealing firearms. The long-range camera lenses of Bluebird Zero Three, who were operating on foot secreted three hundred metres away, zoomed in: each man was in possession of an M1 semi-automatic carbine and a German Walther P99 semi-automatic pistol.

The individual, who appeared to be in charge and giving orders to the group, was the man from the Dover ferry – given the code name Spitfire. It was evident he was proficient in handling weapons and proceeded to instruct the others in firearm's procedure and use. For the next two hours, he put the group through vigorous weapon handling exercises, including firing live rounds at selected targets.

After a short refreshment break, the group leader, Spitfire, took a brick size package from his backpack and placed it on the ground. The others gathered around as he handled the object and gave instruction. The surveillance group identified the package as an explosive device and Spitfire was giving instructions on how to arm it. At the end of the session, during which each member was seen practicing on the device, the group formed a human circle and hugged each other before putting on their backpacks and heading back to the lodge. Bluebird Zero Three remained secreted in situ. The walk back was monitored from the Motherbird, parked five miles away, using the resources of a small radio-controlled drone flying at a height undetectable to the terrorist group.

Earlier in the morning, when the cell had left the lodge heading into Glencoe valley, a three-man surveillance team (Bluebird Zero Two) had made a covert entry into the lodge. The team included an expert on chemical, biological and radioactive warfare who was in possession of electronic detection equipment.

The holdall, seen earlier that morning being carried from the shore, was found in a cupboard. It contained several sealed packages and metal containers with sealed screw tops. The expert's equipment identified the presence of explosives and, more worryingly, from the metal containers a high level of radioactive material. The holdall was left in situ with the contents untouched. The team left the lodge, reporting their findings to Motherbird and Central Command.

By midday, all members of the cell were back in the lodge, sitting together talking and eating lunch. Their monitored conversations clearly identified they felt safe and had no inclination they might be under surveillance, nor that the authorities were aware of their activities and intentions. In fact, every word was being transmitted live back to Motherbird and Central Command.

14:30 hours: Central Command and Motherbird now had detailed knowledge of the cell's intentions: three simultaneous terrorist attacks in the UK. One at the heart of London's financial centre; one at Heathrow Airport and, third at the Houses of Parliament. Delivery would be by radioactive 'dirty-bombs'. They possessed detailed plans and had the materials, weaponry and know-how to succeed. Surveillance monitoring had established they were prepared, if cornered, to use their weapons and die for the cause. And, no doubt, detonate the radioactive devices when doing so.

In the Mercedes control vehicle, parked five miles from the lodge, Jane convened a meeting with the three members of Bluebird Zero Two, to discuss their findings in more detail.

The expert gave his assessment, "On a conservative estimate, the holdall contains about twenty kilos of industrial explosive. It is likely to be Semtex. However, the sealed metal containers cause me the greater concern. Initial readings indicate radioactive caesium chloride."

Jane nervously fiddled with her pen and readied to make notes before asking, "What are the implications?"

The expert smiled and calmly replied, "A dirty-bomb is made of radioactive material attached to conventional explosives. They are sometimes called 'the poor man's nuclear weapon'. In that holdall, there is enough radioactive material and explosives to make at least five significant size dirty bombs. A genuinely concerning prospect."

Jane noted his response and asked, "What exactly is caesium chloride?"

The expert explained, "It is radioactive material which, in the old Soviet Union, was used in seed irradiation. Much of this and other radioactive materials used by the Soviets, are now unaccounted for. No one knows where it is or who has the possession of it. It has long been rumoured that crime syndicates had sold some to terrorist organisations."

Jane looked up from writing her notes and enquired, "And what are the consequences of such a dirty-bomb exploding in London?"

The expert gently tapped on his notebook, "These are not weapons of mass destruction, they are potentially a weapon of mass disruption. A dirty bomb with five kilos of explosive detonated in the financial centre of London could disperse radioactivity over a wide area: Large areas of contamination, resulting in long term sickness such as cancer. A radius of ten miles or more could remain harmful for two hundred years. That is the capability of one bomb, and we have seen in the lodge sufficient material to make four or more."

The group remained silent for a minute or two as they took in what had been said. In response to further questions, the expert explained that transporting and assembling the bombs also presented a danger of explosion and radioactive contamination.

Jane communicated the content of their discussion to Central Command. The cell must not be allowed to leave with the bombs. The consequences of them escaping and achieving their goal, in London or elsewhere, would be catastrophic. The normal means of detention and arrest was not an option for this heavily armed and dangerous terrorist group.

Further intelligence gleaned back in London indicated, this terrorist cell's operation was intended as a first wave attack on three targets – with a second wave, by another group, anticipated within days or weeks.

19:00 hours: The decision has been taken at the very highest level: "Take the group out. Eliminate the danger." Having confirmed that all the terrorists were together in the lodge, the surveillance team was ordered back to the airfield leaving one member, Paul Westbrook, in situ to maintain continuity until Special Forces were fully deployed.

Within minutes of the withdrawal, several dull thuds echoed across the valley: something was wrong. The Special Forces team arrived at the location and transmitted a brief message: "OPERATIVE DOWN. ONE OF YOURS. KILLED BY TERRORISTS. CONTINUING WITH OPERATION TO SECURE THE LODGE."

The outcome of their actions was not discussed nor commented on. Except, at 21:30 hours direction was received for the MOD specialist team to attend the lodge and take possession of the bombs.

By midnight, the lodge was declared CLEAN. No further discussion or explanation was needed. All trace of the terrorist group had been removed: The individuals and their vehicles had vanished. The major terrorist threat had been eliminated and the perpetrators liquidated.

Paul Westbrook, a member of the MI5 team had also been killed: No details of his death would be made public. There would be a confidential internal enquiry. However, few within the service would initially be made aware of his death. In time, his name would appear on the wall memorial, located in the inner sanctum of MI5 HQ, to commemorate officers killed in the course of duty.

The flight back in the Hercules military transport aircraft was a quiet affair. Few words were exchanged. In the dimly light cabin, Lawson looked across at Jane but did not speak: the emptiness in his eyes conveyed his thoughts and concerns.

She gently and slowly shook her head, "Don't ask. They planned evil. Today the good guys have triumphed. Operation Brimstone has been successful and has been closed. Tomorrow is another day." She did not even mention the death of MI5 member Paul Westbrook: one bloody good anonymous guy sacrificed to save hundreds, and with his death, the integrity of the State has been maintained.

The military aircraft with the MI5 team arrived back at Brize Norton airbase during the early hours of the morning. The Special Forces group flew back in their separate military aircraft. On arrival, the MI5 team were taken to the officers' quarters to rest and use the facilities. Lawson noticed that Special Forces bunked out together in the gymnasium, resting on their sleeping bags and not coming into contact with other people. It was a deliberate policy for them to remain elite and isolated.

After having an early breakfast, the MI5 team were asked to meet in the conference hall. Members of Special Forces were already seated at a separate table. None of the group wore any insignia to identify rank or regiment. They were likely to be Special Air Service (22 SAS). However, one individual was clearly in charge and, away from the group, was in quiet conversation with Jane Rigby. Lawson thought he was probably an army colonel. It appeared some form of event was being discussed.

A suited gentleman approached Jane and the colonel. He introduced himself as the private secretary to the Prime Minister and explained that shortly the PM with a couple of Cabinet Ministers would be calling in to "join in the celebrations."

Jane Rigby's response was swift and to the point: "This is not a celebration. Every one of our members is a professional: we undertake what action is required. We do not 'celebrate' killing people. Please refrain from using such words. May I ask that the PM simply thank the team for a successful outcome." The colonel discreetly nodded in agreement.

The PM arrived with his two ministers and other staff. There was minimal formality. They briefly stopped at each of several tables and offered words of thanks. One minister got a little carried away by the occasion and enquired to a member of Special Forces if it were true, they are trained to kill with their bare hands. He clearly was not impressed with the silly question. He remained seated, nodded and in a quiet voice added: "With a single finger." He pointed his right index finger towards the minister and, as if holding an imaginary gun squeezed the trigger quietly voicing 'bang'. Then placed his finger in front of his lips and gently blew. The embarrassed minister walked to the next table. No photographs of the visit were permitted, and it would not be reported in the press.

Several months on from the operation, and following a violent storm out at sea, the wreckage of the yacht involved in delivering the weapons and explosive devices, was found washed up on a remote beach some three hundred mile away. The bodies of the two crew members were never found. The civil authorities recorded the matter as: "Crew presumed dead in an accident at sea."

The mobile telephones recovered by Special Forces from the lodge subsequently provided much valuable intelligence for the security services of the UK and their foreign allies. For a period following the operation, the Security Service kept the mobile telephones active: purporting to be the terrorists when receiving and transmitting communication from their foreign masters. By this means, they were able to identify some of the main players and locate their hideouts in Yemen and elsewhere. Appropriate action was then undertaken to eliminate them.

Finally, DNA taken from the bodies of the terrorists at the lodge resulted in their identification and helped to link them with other known active terrorists operating abroad. The follow-up action prevented the potential for a second wave of attacks on the UK.

The events and consequences of Operation Brimstone were never made public. The Prime Minister and senior members of the Cabinet Office were briefed with an update on the operation and its eventual successful outcome. The case papers on Operation Brimstone remain sealed, marked "Top Secret".

Chapter Eight

Unexplained Death

It was early Monday morning at MI5 London HQ when Jane Rigby called Lawson to her office for a briefing. As he entered, she handed him a thin buff coloured file marked 'Top Secret: Operation Dismount'.

"Julian, an interesting case. I would like you, with Mark Holloway, to review it. The facts are brief but intriguing. The report is from our colleagues at GCHQ. During an electronic surveillance operation, they intercepted 'chatter' from an unknown source in the UK to a foreign site located within Eastern Europe. It indicates a certain target had been 'liquidated' and would cause them no further embarrassment. Currently, we do not know the identity of the sender or receiver. However, we have identified the 'target' as a James Whitehead, recently deceased. The man was fifty-two years of age and the owner of a large country house in West Sussex called Timberland Lodge. He has never before appeared on our radar or known to UK police."

Lawson opened the file and took out a colour aerial photograph of an imposing country house situated within a rural setting of several acres of land.

"That must be worth three million pounds of anyone's money."

Jane nodded.

"Land Registry records show he purchased the property about eight years ago via a local estate agent. It was a cash transaction."

She continued.

"Earlier this morning, at my request, Special Branch ran checks on him and established that, three days ago he suffered an apparent heart attack at his West Sussex home and was pronounced dead on arrival at the Brighton County Hospital."

"So, what is the current police involvement?" enquired Lawson.

"Until our contact with Special Branch, the local police were not treating the death as suspicious. The matter had been left with the coroner to deal. Interestingly, Special Branch reported that although he lived the lifestyle of a millionaire, there is no record to show how he came by his wealth. They have even failed to find a UK bank account in his name. Apparently, a man without a past! He has a younger wife who alleges she doesn't know anything about his finances or his past."

Later that day, Lawson and Holloway drove over the South Downs to the village of Fittleworth and on to a winding lane stopping at the gated entrance of Timberland Lodge. Lawson pressed the buzzer by the intercom. The double metal gates opened without any communication. They drove the two hundred metres to the house and parked next to a silver-coloured Mercedes CLK coupe.

The large oak door to the house was opened by a slim, attractive and smartly dressed woman, with long blonde hair resting on her shoulders.

"I was expecting you. The local policeman said the CID would be calling."

Lawson noted a slight foreign accent, possibly East European. She had assumed they were from the local CID and he was not about to tell her anything different.

"We are sorry to have to trouble you at such a sad time. There are just a few routine questions we need to ask."

She smiled and with a gesture of her hand invited them into the house. The two men were taken into an opulent sitting room with floor to ceiling windows, overlooking extensive gardens with the South Downs in the background.

Lawson judged her to be in her mid-thirties. She did not appear to be grieving for the sudden loss of her husband. With a smile she invited them to take a seat, whilst she made a fresh pot of coffee and disappeared into the kitchen.

Holloway looked at Lawson and both shrugged their shoulders in silent agreement. This was not the expected response of a grieving wife.

Mrs Whitehead returned carrying a silver tray with three white bone china cups, a jug of coffee and a plate of chocolate biscuits which she placed on a low table.

"Please help yourselves."

Lawson opened the conversation, endeavouring to appear informal and not give her the impression the visit was anything other than routine.

"This is a lovely house Mrs Whitehead. I am sorry, but I don't know your first name."

She smiled, "Lara."

"May I call you Lara?"

"Please do."

Lawson poured coffee for the three and sat back on the cream leather sofa.

"Do I detect a slight accent?"

She nodded: "Polish."

He continued, "How did you meet your husband James?"

"I came to England about eight years ago to better my English and was looking for a job when a London employment agency sent me here as a housekeeper."

Holloway asked, "Did James interview you for the position?"

"No, that was left to the agency. I think James had seen my photograph. I knew I had got the job before I arrived."

"So, what happened when you arrived?" asked Holloway.

"I come from a small poor village. So, I was happy and impressed with this lovely English house in the countryside. Just James lived here. I was given my own room and told I would be responsible for looking after the house and cooking meals for him. At first, he was not very friendly and did not talk to me much. He seemed a lonely man."

"So how did the relationship develop?" Lawson enquired.

Lara sat back on the other large cream leather sofa, tucking her slender legs underneath her, and answered his question.

"It wasn't very romantic. After a couple of months, he just said he liked me living here and suggested I should be his wife. We never actually got married. From that day I began to use his surname."

Lawson looked quizzical, smiled and leaned forward.

"I am intrigued, please explain more."

Lara unfolded her legs and in an almost teasing manner, leaned towards him.

"Look, I recently arrived in the UK with no qualifications and limited English. My expectations were that I would be working as a cleaner or picking vegetables in some cold wet field in Norfolk. Yet here I was, working in a lovely house with the promise of security and more money than I had ever dreamed of having. It was not a difficult decision. He said I could keep my own room and maybe, once a week, he would come in for sex and then leave."

Holloway asked, "Did you love him?"

"Love didn't come into it. It was convenient for both. He was never unkind, and I respected him."

"Were you frightened of him?" asked Lawson.

"A little. He was the boss."

Still leaning forward, and in a gentle voice, he continued.

"How was the relationship convenient for James?"

Lara held her hands together and looked at her nails.

"He never explained why. I have always thought he was trying to hide his wealth from the tax man. He only dealt in cash and he had lots of it. On the day I became Mrs Lara Whitehead, he insisted I open a bank account in that name. The household accounts were all in my name and I was responsible for paying the bills. Each month, James would give me three thousand pounds in cash to be put in my account. From that I would pay the bills and buy whatever I needed."

"Just household bills?" enquired Holloway.

"No, sometimes much bigger items. When he bought his new Mercedes, he gave me the cash and I visited the car showrooms and purchased it in my name."

Lawson asked, "So as Mr & Mrs Whitehead please explain your life together. What was his work? Your social life? His attitude towards you?"

"He never discussed work. He never discussed anything. I knew my place and quickly learned not to ask questions. He was often busy in his study," she said pointing to a room at the end of the sitting room. "Often he would go out in his car and sometimes be away for several days. He always had his large black leather brief case with him and kept his paperwork, laptop and mobile phone in it."

Lawson interrupted, "Did he make calls from the home phones?"

"Never. He never used nor answered the phone. If the phone rang, I would have to answer it. I cannot recall ever taking a call from someone asking for him. Occasionally, he would take a call on his mobile but would then go into his study to answer it."

"Please continue," said Lawson.

"A couple of time each year he would take me to London, to the theatre or a restaurant but never with others. He said he did not like mixing with people. James was generous and would buy me expensive presents when in London. Payment for everything was in cash. We never travelled abroad. I often shop in the village and in the local towns, but James never did."

Lawson stood up and walked around the room, using the opportunity to make a mental note of the security sensors on the windows and patio doors before turning to Lara.

"You say he was the boss. How did he show that?"

Lara gave a slight smile.

"He was in charge. On the day I became Mrs Whitehead, he took my passport and said he would look after things. I assumed he would sort out my long term stay in the UK. It was never again discussed. He said, I must not contact friends or relatives back home in Poland and I was not permitted to have anyone back to the house. I wasn't allowed a mobile phone or a computer."

"And you readily accepted such restrictions?" asked Lawson.

"It was a small price to pay for my new life of luxury. He was keen that the people in the village knew me as Mrs Whitehead. However, he was extremely strict that I did not tell them anything about him except, if asked, to say he was terribly busy and often abroad on business."

Holloway said, "I must compliment you on your English."

Lara replied, "James was very generous, he paid for me to attend English classes at Brighton College."

Lawson asked, "Did James ever had visitors to the house?"

"Never."

"Not even friends or family?"

"No. In all my time with him I was never introduced to any friend or relative."

"Didn't you find that strange?" Lawson enquired.

Lara shrugged her shoulders.

"I played by his rules. He did not like socialising. I considered myself fortunate he liked me."

Lawson said, "From what you have said, I am assuming you have never applied for UK citizenship. What do you consider your legal statue to be?"

For the first time Lara showed signs of concern in her voice.

"I am not sure."

Lawson responded with reassurance.

"Please don't be concerned. It can be sorted."

He continued in a gentle tone.

"I note there are no photographs displayed neither in this room nor in the hall. Why is that?"

Lara replied, "Another one of James's dislikes. He did not own a camera and would not allow me to have one. I don't have a single photograph of him."

Lawson sat back down.

"Lara, without wishing you distress, what happened on the day James fell ill?"

Lara looked thoughtful.

"He'd been out most of the day. Last Friday returning at 4 pm, I heard his car on the driveway and went to meet him at the front door. James said he had chest pains and felt unwell. He did not say where he had been but seemed a little confused and angry. He poured himself a large whisky and sat down to watch television. I went back to the kitchen when I heard him scream out my name twice. I ran into the sitting room. He was on the floor clutching his chest, and then he went limp. I dialled 999 for an ambulance and rushed to his side. He had stopped breathing. The ambulance arrived within about fifteen minutes and worked on him, but he was pronounced dead when he arrived at hospital."

Lawson asked, "If we may have a look in his briefcase, it might help establish where he had been during the day and account for any stress he may have been under." It was a rouse to find any information about the man.

Lara shook her head.

"When he came in, he wasn't carrying his briefcase. He left home with it. It could be in his car."

Without further comment, she walked into the hall towards the driveway where the Mercedes was parked. Lawson turned to Holloway and pointing towards the study mouthed "Check it out. Two minutes," before following Lara. Holloway nodded in acknowledgement.

Lara unlocked the car and together they examined the interior and the boot. There was no sign of the briefcase. Lawson noted a lack of any documents or identifying items in the vehicle: It was as clean as the day it had left the dealer's showroom.

He walked slowly around the car appearing to admire the quality, but with a more professional interest.

"It's a lovely looking vehicle. Do you ever drive it?"

"No."

"The number plates suggest it is only a few months old."

"Yes, we bought it new six months ago," replied Lara.

Lawson was interested in the car.

They walked back into the hall with Lawson discretely noting the security system, the location of the control panel and the brand name of the equipment. There was an absence of a CCTV system.

Holloway came into the hall to meet them.

Turning to Lara Lawson said, "We are finished for now. May I once again offer you our sincere condolences? The Coroner's Officer will be in touch to discuss the details of the inquest etc."

Both men shook her hand and began to walk towards their car. Lara remained at the entrance watching their progress.

Lawson turned to Holloway.

"You must first have a look at this beautiful car" and gently guided him towards the Mercedes.

In a quieter voice he continued, "This car interests me. The interior is as clean as a whistle. No documents, no maps. Not even a chocolate wrapper."

Holloway replied, "His study is just the same. As sterile as a new show house. Expensive furnishings, but nothing about him. No diary, no files and no photographs. Not even a telephone or computer on the desk. The in-tray only contains household bills in Lara's name. His jacket was on the back of the chair, but no wallet. Pockets clean except for a gold money clip containing, I would estimate, a couple of grand. Plus, a single Yale door key and a Parker ballpoint pen."

Aware that Lara was still watching from a distance. Lawson continued in a low voice.

"Mark, this car is only six months old, yet the speedometer shows over ten thousand miles. What has this man been doing and where has he been going?"

Holloway smiled, "Let us get Special Branch to undertake an ANPR (Automatic number plate recognition) check. No doubt much of his travels would have been undertaken on main roads and motorways where the system operates."

Walking to the rear of the car, Lawson responded, "I don't think it will be that easy. We are dealing with a professional at the top of his game, whatever his game is. Do you notice any tail-tail signs?"

Holloway shook his head.

"Look at the lower half of the car and the number plate," encouraged Lawson. "The lower half shows the grime and dust from everyday motorway and country road driving. Yet, look carefully at the number plate. It is clean. No mud splatters or dust. The front plate is in the same condition."

Holloway raised his eyebrows and looked at him.

Lawson continued.

"I've taken a closer look at both number plates and on each there are tiny faint square indentations. This indicates to me, the vehicle has been driven using magnetic false number plates over the originals."

Holloway nodded in agreement. They turned and walked across to their car.

Lara remained at the front door, waving goodbye. The two men drove off down the drive and onto the country lane. Holloway was driving.

"What do you make of her?" he asked.

"She is either very naive or very clever," responded Lawson. "I'll reserve judgement for the present as to whether she is the genuine article. We will need to run some in-depth background checks on her."

"And what do you make of the mysterious late Mr Whitehead?" asked Holloway.

Lawson bit his lower lip.

"Yes, what do we know about the late Mr Whitehead? Very little, but we can be certain he was not born James Whitehead. It is a long shot, but I was wondering if he may have once been a police 'super-grass' and, having given court evidence against dangerous criminals, acquired lifetime immunity and protection in accordance with the Police Witness Protection Programme. From my experience, it has many of the elements. However, the establishment isn't normally that generous with its money."

"It's an area we need to close down and also check that he wasn't being looked after by any of our agencies or cousins across the pond," responded Holloway.

Lawson smiled and nodded.

"I'll include it as an action in my report."

En-route back to Head Quarters, little was said between the two men. Lawson sat with his laptop typing the report which, over a secure internet connection, he sent electronically to Jane Rigby.

It was late evening when the two men arrived back at the office. Jane had read the report and was waiting for them. She had already instigated basic checks on Lara and the deceased and had the results in front of her.

"Special Branch has given me categorical assurance that your man is not known to the UK police and was not on the Police Protection Programme. And he was not being 'babysat' by any of our sister organisations or cousins."

She continued, "Home Office records confirm a Lara Zamoyski came to the UK from Poland eight years ago to work. As Poland is a member of the European Economic Area, she did not need a visa. However, no further contact with her was had. She became one of the hundreds of thousands of immigrants who just disappeared. There is no photograph of her on record."

"And what about the explanation she gave us?" asked Lawson.

"All the utility services for the house, including council tax, have her down as the account holder. She does not have a National Health number and is not registered with a GP or local dentist. She does not possess a UK driving licence. Her bank account checks out, currently in credit to the tune of over fifty thousand pounds. It was opened by her within two months of arriving in the UK. The details she gave you about paying in three thousand pounds cash each month and settling all the household bills is confirmed. Clearly she was able to keep a little back for her savings."

Lawson walked to the coffee percolator and poured out three mugs of fresh coffee, handing one to each colleague.

"Jane, may I ask that you arrange tasking for further detailed checks on Lara whilst Mark and I continue delving into the background of James Whitehead."

"Yes, of course."

Lawson continued, "We have no clear picture on the true identity of the man James Whitehead or what his game was. Was he a big time criminal or an active member of a hostile foreign intelligence agency? We just do not know. But he was good, very good. He was well trained to the highest professional level. That suggests official sponsorship from an elite source, likely to be a foreign government. At the time of his death, was he still working for them or had he gone rogue?"

Rigby sat in her swivel chair with her arms folded, moving slowly from side to side contemplating the situation.

"There is a contradiction here. The methods he employed to hide his true identity fits in with 'deep cover' training and practices of a hostile agency. However, a 'plant' would normally be housed in an anonymous semi-detached in suburbia. I can't envisage an intelligence director sitting in deepest Moscow, or similar, financing an agent to live the lifestyle of a millionaire."

Lawson added, "I think we can agree he was well trained in the dark art, but where did he get that knowledge and training? Lara says he spoke with an English accent but, in this game, we know foreign 'plants' are trained to pass as UK nationals. At present, there is nothing to say whether he was a rogue operator from one of our security agencies."

He got to his feet and taking the coffee jug, filled his empty mug, before turning to Jane.

"So, who was he? What has he been doing for the past eight years? Why was he so fastidious in keeping in the shadows? How was he getting his money? And did he die from natural causes or was he murdered? The intelligence from GCHQ indicates that he was murdered to be kept silent."

Holloway gestured to Lawson for his mug to be refilled.

"Mark, do you think he was keeping a low profile to hide his activities from the UK security agencies or was he a man on the run and hiding, in fear for his life, from a foreign agency?"

Jane Rigby interjected, "The UK's open-door approach to rich foreigners has, in recent years, been a cause of concern for us. London is awash with billionaires from the former Soviet republics. They are not all on friendly terms with each other and disputes are known to be settled by liquidation."

Holloway raised his mug, "Care for a polonium-laced tea comrade."

He was referring to the case of Alexander Litvinenko, an ex-KGB officer who died a slow and painful death having been poisoned with radioactive Polonium-210. Media reports speculated that he had been working for MI6 and his drink had been laced with the poison by a former Moscow colleague he had met in a London restaurant.

Rigby was not amused.

"Julian, the post-mortem on Whitehead is scheduled for 2 pm. tomorrow at the Brighton City mortuary. Special Branch have made the arrangements. The death has been recorded as sudden and unexplained. A senior Home Office pathologist will undertake the examination. He is on the restricted list and has been made aware of our interest. Please attend as our representative."

Turning to Holloway she added, "Urine samples taken from the corpse earlier today confirm he was not poisoned by a radioactive substance."

He nodded.

Still looking at Holloway she continued, "Mark, tomorrow please stay in the office and undertake further research into the background of the deceased. Full checks: national and international."

Leaning forward in her chair, she turned a couple of pages of the open file before looking up to address Lawson.

"A full detailed and forensic search of the house will be undertaken. I have arranged for a covert team from Special Operations to go in at 8 am tomorrow. I have given them details of the security system."

Lawson raised his right thumb in acknowledgement.

She continued, "A Special Branch officer has already contacted Lara. He will collect her just before eight and take her to the mortuary to view the body. Then back to the police station for a witness statement. She has been told he is local CID and that identification of the body and the taking of a statement is normal procedure. He will ensure she is not returned home until midday."

Rigby handed Lawson a sealed A4 envelope.

"Julian, I'd like you to go in with the team. Contact details are in here. The time frame will allow you to then go on to the city mortuary for the post-mortem."

Chapter Nine
Covert Entry

The unmarked police car drove slowly from Timberland Lodge down the driveway to the electronic double metal gates, stopping momentarily for them to open. Lara, seated in the front passenger seat, looked relaxed and was talking to the detective driver. It was exactly 8 am. The car turned left and sped off in the direction of Brighton.

The small red Royal Mail van, parked near the junction of the lane, did not seem out of place in this rural location. The driver appeared to be sorting through a bundle of envelopes in his hands. He looked up and pressed a button on the van's console.

"Target has departed. Clear to proceed."

Within seconds, a white Ford Transit van drew up at the closing gates. The Special Operations Unit had arrived.

The front seat passenger leaned out of the open window and pointed a device at the gate's electronic mechanism. They came to a sudden stop and re-opened. The van proceeded slowly towards the house, parking with its rear within two metres of the main front door.

The back doors of the van opened. Two men dressed in dark blue overalls and wearing tool belts stepped down and walked briskly out of sight to the rear of the house. Within a minute the front door of the house was opened from inside. One of the men was standing in the hallway smiling.

"Security systems neutralised. It is safe to enter."

Eight further operatives walked quickly from the back of the van into the hallway. All were wearing blue overalls with tool belts. Some carried aluminium cases containing electronic and forensic equipment. Lawson was the last person out of the van. The driver remained in the vehicle as the communications officer.

In the confines of the hallway each put on white disposable gloves and overshoes. The team leader handed out floor plans of the house. Each member had prearranged functions to undertake. Without further conversation, they dispersed to undertake their specific tasks. The unit was highly trained in covert entry and bypass techniques of locks, safes and security systems. Sensitive 'intrusions' to gather information required the signed authority of a senior government minister.

Before conducting a physical search of the property, each area was subjected to an electronic sweep to ascertain the possible presence of transmitting or recording devices. None was found. The search was undertaken in a methodical and meticulous fashion. Only one cupboard or drawer was opened at a time and carefully returned to its former position. Likewise, only one piece of furniture or picture frame was moved at a time and then replaced before another was touched.

Every inch of the property including the loft space, double-garage and outbuildings were searched and forensically examined but, apart from the study, nothing of relevance was found.

The team leader met with Lawson in the hallway.

"Julian, we've found nothing to establish the true identity of the deceased or what he was up to. In six years of doing this work, I've never come across such a sterile living environment."

"Interestingly, in the study wall safe we have found Lara's Polish passport and the Deeds to the house, which are in the name James Whitehead, but no other documentation," responded Lawson.

The team leader raised his right index finger and smiled.

"And the little matter of one hundred and fifty thousand pounds in new Bank of England notes, plus an American silver dollar. Possibly it is a lucky charm. The only other paperwork in the study is a copy of last Wednesday's edition of the Daily Telegraph in the wastepaper bin. No files, books or magazines. Nothing."

Lawson queried, "When Mark Holloway checked the study, there was a jacket with a wad of cash and a single Yale door key."

The team leader interrupted, "Both still in situ and we have taken an impression of the key. It doesn't fit any lock in the house."

"And how about Lara's room?" enquired Lawson.

The team leader shrugged his shoulders.

"A similar story. Nothing found to identify a link with her past or a shred of information about any contacts or friends she may have acquired since she took up residence here some eight years ago. Just a few receipts from London shops relating to the purchase of jewellery."

The two men walked into the sitting room and the team leader continued.

"Lara has her own bedroom and en-suite bathroom. She is certainly living in luxury and materially does not want for anything. The clothing is all expensive brands. Her bookshelf shows a liking for Dickens and Jane Austen and her taste in music is for the Classics."

Lawson walked to the patio doors and looked out across to the South Downs in the distance and then turned to the team leader.

"The lack of evidence speaks volumes. It is evidence that something is really wrong, if that makes sense."

The team leader looked at his watch.

"It's eleven-fifteen and we are about finished. Everything has been photographed and everything left in situ. DNA swabs have been taken from Lara's toothbrush and from her hairbrush. Plus, finger mark lifts from items in her bedroom. As your Boss requested, my lads have also installed electronic eavesdropping devices and cameras in the house, which will be monitored from HQ."

Lawson looked at him with a quizzical gaze.

"Isn't that dangerous? We do not know much about either the deceased or Lara. At least one of them was a professional. Wouldn't it cause the service an embarrassment if the house were swept by the 'enemy' and our devices were found?"

The team leader shook his head and smiled broadly.

"All our devices are made in-house. None of the elements, bar one, can be traced. That one item we 'acquire' from a hostile country, usually Russia or China. Let me give you an example."

He walked around the room and continued in his explanation.

"A couple of years ago, we installed an eavesdropping device in the London home of a Russian billionaire. Recently, he was having problems with some of his old colleagues and was not sure who he could trust. At great expense, he had flown in from America a top team of private specialists to sweep his home. Our bug was found and analysed. It contained an element only manufactured for use by the Russian Security Service. Convinced Mr Putin's boys were after him, he came to us. And is now a particularly useful source of intelligence."

Lawson shook his head and walked towards the hallway.

"I still have a lot to learn."

The team leader summoned his group into the hallway, where each removed their disposable gloves and footwear and placed them into a plastic sack before climbing into the parked Transit van. Two members remained kitted-up in the hallway. These were the 'cleaners'. They would now re-visit each room and meticulously check that nothing had been left out of place or any equipment had been left behind and that no alien mark had been left on any surface.

Finally, the front door of the house was closed with all members of the team back in the van. The front seat passenger pointed a device in the direction of the house.

"House secure. Security system reset."

The team leader nodded to Lawson.

"Not even the most astute person would detect anyone had been in the house."

A small red light flashed on the console of the still parked Royal Mail van. The driver checked the road and then pressed a button.

"Road all clear. Safe to proceed."

The white Transit van exited the driveway and dropped Lawson off at a nearby motorway service station. His next port of call was the Brighton City mortuary.

Chapter Ten
The Post-Mortem

The Brighton City mortuary is a single-storey Victorian red brick and flint faced building, with high small frosted glass windows. It is discreetly located behind the crematorium at the far end of the city's main cemetery. A large red sign displayed on the single external door reads NO UNAUTHORISED ACCESS. There is no signage to identify the building's function.

Lawson pressed the brass buzzer and waited. The door was opened by a middle-aged man, small of statue, dressed in white protective clothing and a blue plastic apron which nearly touched the floor. As he walked, it flapped against his yellow surgical wellington boots. He did not speak but simply gestured Lawson to follow him.

The walls and floor of the outer reception area consisted of white and green pattern tiles, with a variety of large yellow Health & Safety signs displayed on each wall. The air was chilly, with the distinct smell of death and disinfectant. It reminded Lawson of his youth and frequent school visits to the local Victorian public swimming baths in Brighton.

The man in the yellow boots locked the door behind him and, again without speaking, pointed in the direction of the main office.

It was 1:45 pm. Lawson was the last to arrive.

Professor Nicholas Forbes was seated in an old, leather armchair in the far corner, reading his case notes. A tall slim dour man, with a ruddy complexion, wearing half-rimmed spectacles: A distinguished pathologist at the height of his profession. He did not look up. Norma, the middle-aged mortuary technician, was busy serving coffee and chatting to the police photographer, the coroner's officer and the scenes of crime exhibits officer. She had held the position for many years and was well known to, and respected by, the local police.

As Lawson entered, Norma smiled and handed him a cup of coffee.

"Help yourself to biscuits."

He noted the professor was drinking from a bone china cup, whereas everyone else had standard light green government issue cups. Normally, Norma supplied plain Digestive biscuits but today they were chocolate Digestives. He smiled to himself: *She is out to impress the professor*.

Through the open-door Lawson saw the assistant in yellow boots pushing a trolley, on which was positioned a body, through the double swing doors into the Post-mortem Room. Norma looked up.

"Professor, the body has been stripped and washed. We will be ready to go in ten minutes."

Lawson enquired to view the clothing and items taken from the deceased. The assistant carried it in a plastic box and laid out the items on a side table. Lawson quickly examined them, took photographs and made a written record:

1.   Alexander McQueen handcrafted black leather lace up shoes, size 9.
2.   Alfred Dunhill light blue shirt, size 16.
3.   Ralph Lauren pinstripe suit trousers, waist 36.
4.   Marks and Spencer black socks and underwear.
5.   Gent's Rolex wristwatch (Oyster Daytona) with black crocodile strap.
6.   Cartier silver cufflinks.
7.   Gold signet ring with oval black onyx stone.
8.   Gold wedding band.

Lawson thought: Here is a man who has the money to lavish luxury on himself and keen to promote his image. Yet, the M & S items indicate 'if not seen', wear practical and value for money clothing.

He noted the wedding ring had worn thin, suggesting many years of use, whereas the watch and other jewellery items were in relatively new condition. He recorded the serial number of the watch and the hallmarking's of the other items.

The professor strolled over to Lawson.

"Going outside for a smoke before we begin. Care to join me?"

Together they walked into the rear yard.

Looking over the top of his spectacles and rolling a cigarette between his fingers the professor looked, with a wry smile, across at Lawson.

"Mr Lawson, representing HM Government? Last time we met was on the Michael White murder investigation post-mortem. Then it was DCI Ben Swan. Different name. Different department!"

Lawson laughed.

"Life is a game. And I appear destined to play many parts. I'm on a two-year secondment with the secret squirrels."

"So, who was this guy?" asked the professor.

"At present, we have few leads. He has been in Sussex for eight years, living the life of a millionaire, but we do not know where he is from, what he has been doing or how he has come by his wealth. He has taken extraordinary steps to cover his tracks and only came to our notice because an intelligence source says he was liquidated. Test on his urine sample confirms that he was not poisoned by a radioactive substance."

The professor laughed.

"Well, it's good to know I am not going to cut into a radioactive body."

The two men walked back into the Receiving Room to join the others. Each member put on a white disposable protective suit with hood, white surgical wellington boots and a double set of latex gloves and then walked through a disinfectant foot bath, before entering the post-mortem theatre. The swing doors were locked from the inside. An illuminated sign over the top of the door read: NO ENTRY. POSTMORTEM IN PROGRESS.

The naked body was laid out on the stainless-steel post-mortem table. Under the direction of the professor the photographer took photographs of the body and then stepped back. The professor switched on his voice activated microphone which was attached to a cord around his neck.

Walking slowly around the body he described out loud what he was seeing:

"White male, approximately 50 years of age. Height five ten. Weight approximately twelve and a half stone. No visible external injury. No bruising. No unusual marks. Faint scaring to indicate vasectomy, but many years ago."

He then held and examined each arm and hand, running his right hand carefully from the tips of the deceased's fingers to the shoulder, he stated, "No defensive injury or damage to arms or hands."

Next, he asked the assistant to turn the body onto its side.

"No injury or marks to head or back. In conclusion, no external evidence to indicate a violent death."

Turning to the other members present, the professor gave a faint smile.

"Everyone ready? Then let us begin."

A trolley of stainless-steel equipment, including scalpels and cutting tools, was wheeled to his right side.

The chest cavity was cut open. Each vital organ was carefully removed, dissected and examined before being placed into a stainless-steel bowl being held by Norma, the mortuary technician. In turn, she carried each organ to an electronic set of scales for weighing before writing the result up on a whiteboard on the wall. A small sample was sliced from each organ and placed into an exhibits container and sealed.

Various fluids, together with hair samples, nail clippings and DNA swabs were taken for further analysis.

The detailed post-mortem examination had taken just over three hours. The professor reported finding: no signs of internal injuries or evidence that physical force had been used to cause the death.

He found no sign of heart disease to suggest a heart attack having been brought on by natural causes.

Glancing across to Lawson, the professor pointed to the open mouth of the deceased.

"Take a good look in there. Extensive and expensive dentistry work with implants and crowns. It is good but, I would suggest, not the work of a UK or American trained dentist. We need to get a forensic dentist from the Department of Odontology to have a look."

On the professor's instructions, plastic bags containing the various organs were placed into the chest cavity. The ribs were pulled closed and the chest was stitched up by the mortuary assistant. Whilst this was being undertaken, the scenes of crime officer took fingerprints from the body.

As is his custom, when the professor had completed his formal examination and exploration, he stepped back and slowly walked around the body. He meticulously re-examined every detail occasionally touching, with his index finger, an area of the skin.

After a few silent minutes, he gave a faint smile and pursed his lips in a quizzical manner. Pointing to the lower rear section of the right calf, he half turned to his audience.

"What do you make of that?"

The scenes of crime officer leaned forward to look.

"A small mole, I would imagine."

The professor took a small torch from his breast pocket and from a distance of a few inches shone it onto the mole.

"Notice anything strange?" There was no reply.

He handed his torch to Lawson.

"Have a careful look."

Whilst Lawson was viewing the 'mole' the professor commented with a smile, "Ever seen a mole that reflects light? Whatever is secreted just under the skin, is metallic and probably man made."

The professor leaned forward and with a pair of tweezers, delicately removed the small metal object and placed it into a plastic exhibit bottle. The object had the appearance of a tinny ball-bearing. He moved closer to Lawson and quietly mouthed.

"Are you thinking what I am thinking?"

Lawson nodded and quietly replied.

"Let us discuss this later."

The major significance of the discovery, and the implications, were obvious to both men.

Leaving the post-mortem theatre, the two men each collected a cup of coffee and strolled into the rear garden where they could talk without being overheard. The professor had in his pocket the small exhibit bottle containing the ball-bearing like object. He handed it to Lawson to view.

The object was the size of a pin head and on a close examination he could see two holes drilled through it. Both men were aware of an incident in London many years earlier, when a Bulgarian dissident was assassinated by a poison pellet being injected into his leg by an umbrella being carried by an unknown man.

Lawson commented, "I must get this back to HQ as soon as possible for the forensic examination and to brief the team."

Lawson directed for the body to remain in the 'fridge' at the mortuary. Having taken possession of the jewellery items, he then texted London HQ with an update and asked for a briefing to be arranged.

Later that evening, he met with Jane Rigby and several members of the team. The discovery of the pellet had significantly upgraded the investigation. An intelligence officer gave an overview of the 'umbrella assassination':

Georgi Markov was a Bulgarian dissident writer, who defected and came to live in the UK. He worked as a broadcaster and journalist for the BBC World Service. In September 1978, he was standing at a bus stop when he felt a slight sharp pain, as if a 'bug' bite, on the back of his right thigh. On looking around, he noted a man walking away carrying an umbrella but, at the time, thought little of it. Later that evening he developed a fever and was admitted to hospital. Three days later he died at the age of forty-nine.

Fortunately, he had told the doctors of the umbrella incident and the 'sting' mark on his leg. Scotland Yard ordered a thorough autopsy, and a spherical metal pellet the size of a pinhead was found embedded in the victim's calf. Experts from Porton Down, the Government's Military Science Establishment, identified the object contained traces of ricin. A sugary substance coated the tiny holes which trapped the ricin inside the cavities. The coating was designed to melt on reaching body temperature. Therefore, once injected the ricin was absorbed into the bloodstream and killed Markova. There is no known antidote to ricin. The 'gas gun umbrella' method of assassination has also been recorded on other occasions within Europe.

The exhibit bottle containing the pellet, taken from the body of the deceased James Whitehead, was dispatched by secure courier to Porton Down for forensic analysis and the team adjourned for the day.

In his career in the police, Lawson had attended many post-mortems, but he never got used to the morbid smell it left on his clothing and the unpleasant taste on his lips. From London he would drive straight home, place his clothing in a bag for dry cleaning and have a long soak in a deep hot bath.

Chapter Eleven

The Truth Unravels

During the next three days extensive research and background checks were undertaken into the deceased James Whitehead and Lara.

On the fourth day, the team gathered at their London HQ office to discuss progress. Lawson was the first to report back on the Mercedes car belonging to the deceased.

"When I first examined the car, I suggested it had been using cloned stick-on number plates to avoid detection by the police ANPR (Automatic number plate recognition) system. I am now certain that was the case. The car has covered over ten thousand miles in just six months, yet nowhere in the UK does it appear on ANPR. The system is installed on most UK motorways and many main roads. It is not feasible the car was never clocked."

Cloning is the term used when a criminal identifies an exact match to the car in his possession. This is often achieved by researching the Auto-Trader website or a similar motoring magazine. He then has a false set of number plates of that vehicle made up which he fits to his own car. Thus, there are then two cars travelling around with identical number plates.

By this method, the criminal aims to ensure he is never caught for any motoring violation or criminal activity.

Lawson detailed the research undertaken.

"According to Lara he left home early on the Thursday morning and arrived home at about 4 pm. With this in mind, I asked the ANPR people to review their system, for that eight-hour period, for all silver Mercedes 'clocked' using motorways and main road leaving and entering Sussex. The results are interesting."

Lawson produced a chart and placed it on the whiteboard.

"During that eight-hour period, over one thousand 'hits' for silver Mercedes were captured on ANPR. From these, just over two hundred registered as having both left and then re-entered Sussex."

He produced a typed list.

"This details each of the two hundred vehicles with the name and address of the respective registered keeper. Most have local Sussex addresses. For the moment I am putting these to one side."

Jane Rigby asked, "What's the rationale for doing that?"

Lawson replied, "If fitting false plates, I suggest, the criminal wouldn't pick the registration number of a local car for fear the genuine owner might see him driving around."

Rigby nodded in agreement.

Lawson continued.

"As a first roll of the dice, I drew a line across the country just below Birmingham. This identified twelve cars with registered keepers residing in Birmingham or above. Urgent requests were sent to local police for all twelve to be visited to establish whether their car had been in Sussex on that day. Eleven confirmed 'Yes.' One came back 'No.'

"The 'No' response was from a man residing in Great Harwood, Lancashire. The local Special Branch confirmed he is a respected well-known businessman. His car was registered new from a Manchester based Mercedes dealership and used locally as a demonstrator. The current owner purchased it from them about six months ago. He commutes each day from home to his office in nearby Bolton. Since its purchase, the car has travelled less than three thousand miles and has not travelled further south than Manchester."

Lawson put up on the whiteboard the registration number of the car.

"The next stage, which is already underway, is to run the number through the entire UK ANPR system, plus checks against all databases relating to traffic offences and parking tickets. From that, the Analysts will prepare a schedule to show for each day when, where and which direction our 'cloned' car was travelling."

Jane interjected.

"To summarise: When we identify an incident where it is believed Mr Whitehead was involved, we will be able to consult the schedule to establish if his car was in the vicinity."

Lawson then reported on the enquiries that he had undertaken in respect of the watch and jewellery belonging to the deceased.

"The Rolex watch has a serial number which is registered at the company's main office. It was purchased twelve months ago from a shop in New Bond Street, London. It cost thirteen thousand two hundred pounds and was a cash deal. Details of the purchaser were not recorded."

Rigby interrupted.

"Is it usual to pay cash for such a large sum and not take personal details from the owner?"

"Yes. Increasingly, the new wealthy in London pay in cash and decline their personal details."

Lawson continued.

"From the hallmarks in the gold signet ring and the silver cufflinks, we can state they were made no longer than two years ago. The gold wedding band does not contain UK hallmarks. The indications are it was made from Russian gold. It is well worn and estimated to be about twenty years old."

Holloway then took to the floor to present an update on his research.

"Mrs Lara Whitehead nee Zamoyski! The employment agency that allegedly sent her to James Whitehead is no longer in existence. Apart from the bank account in her name, which may I remind you has a credit balance of over fifty thousand pounds and the utility bills, we have not found her on any other UK database."

He then put up on the screen photographs taken of the receipts found in her bedroom during the covert search.

"All have been checked out. Only one produced a hit. Regarding the Cartier watch, I have visited the London shop in New Bond Street and can confirm it was sold almost two years ago for six thousand seven hundred pounds for cash. Like Mr Whitehead's Rolex watch, the customer did not give personal details."

He then smiled.

"But the gods are on our side. The shop has excellent CCTV facilities with video recordings kept for five years. With the time and date on the receipt, their security man was able to find video of the couple purchasing the watch."

Holloway tapped his laptop and a CCTV video taken from the inside of the shop began.

"This is the couple examining several watches with Lara eventually selecting the one she wanted. She looks excited at the prospect of owning a Cartier watch."

After a pause he continued.

"And now we have James Whitehead taking the cash out of his wallet and handing it to the sales executive."

Lawson jumped to his feet waving his right hand in excitement.

"Hold it there, Mark, just there."

Holloway paused the video.

"What's wrong?"

Lawson tapped into his iPad and carrying it walked towards the wall screen. He carefully looked at the still photograph and then to his iPad before turning to show his audience.

"The man in the shop with Lara is not the man we have in the mortuary. Look carefully at both photographs. The facial features are quite different. The hairline is different. It is not the same man."

Rigby sat back in her chair.

"Interesting. Interesting and significant. Some unknown man paying out over six thousand for her watch. He must be a good friend! Possibly a secret lover?"

Holloway tapped the play button.

"Let me show you the end of the video. Watch the couple leave the shop. Note they get into a car parked outside. She is the driver. It is a blue Audi A3. Unfortunately, we are unable to see the registration number. I've checked with the local council, but the video from their street cameras is no longer in existence."

Rigby looked intently at the screen.

"But we were given to understand Lara couldn't drive."

Lawson still standing commented.

"That's what she indicated to us and there is no record at DVA (Driver & Vehicle Agency) of her having a UK drivers' licence. This lady has questions to answer."

Holloway walked and stood next to Lawson and continued his presentation.

"There is more to ponder. For eight years, this attractive lady has lived in luxury but on a very restrictive rein. With her older 'husband' dead, wouldn't you expect her to immediately contact family back home or rush out to buy the latest mobile phone and computer he had deprived her of having? But she doesn't."

He walked back to the desk and took out a report from his folder.

"Since our equipment was installed, Special Operations have monitored Lara at home. She has not phoned anyone nor had a single visitor to the house. Each morning begins with a forty-five-minute workout in the gym followed by housework to the strains of Verdi, then mid-morning she cycles to the village shops to buy fresh provisions before returning home for an early lunch. Then it is reading and watching television before early to bed. She appears totally happy and unconcerned about the future."

Rigby then dropped a potential game changer.

"Just before this meeting began, I received a note. Delicate enquiries by our colleagues operating in Poland state Lara Zamoyski, with the same date of birth and home address as given in the passport found in the wall safe, is still resident in Poland. Further enquiries are in hand. So, who is our Lara Whitehead?"

"I suggest we undertake a further visit to flush her out," commented Lawson.

Chapter Twelve

The Grieving Wife

The decision was made for Lawson to make a solo visit to Timberland Lodge to see Lara on the pretext that he was concerned for her well-being. Special Operations were directed to continue monitoring her movements in the house and have a team on standby should she leave. Surveillance had established Lara's daily routine. Lawson decided he would attempt to meet her as she returned from her morning visit to the local shops.

It was a fresh, bright and sunny early August morning, when he parked his car in the nearby lay-by and waited. Within ten minutes, a voice message was received on his covert radio.

"Target will be at the gates within the minute."

Lawson turned the ignition on and slowly cruised along the lane towards Timberland Lodge. Lara came into view peddling towards the gates on her old fashion style stand-up cycle. They met at the gates.

"Hello Lara. How fortuitous. I was just passing and thought I'd call in to see how you were coping and to offer any help."

She smiled, "That is very kind of you. Do join me for coffee."

Lara dismounted from her cycle and activated the electronic gates to open. They walked together along the driveway towards the house. She appeared relaxed.

Lawson noted the basket on the front of the cycle was filled with fresh vegetables, bread and a copy of the Daily Telegraph.

As Lara unlocked the front door, Lawson picked up the contents from the basket and followed her into the house.

She turned to him.

"Let's have coffee in the kitchen, its warmer and cosy there."

In keeping with the rest of the house, it was a top-quality oak fitted kitchen with a central island and black granite worktops. He deposited the goods on the central island and sat down on a leather chair. Lara prepared a fresh jug of coffee and sat opposite him.

"The post-mortem hasn't yet produced a positive outcome. They are waiting for the laboratory results," said Lawson. He deliberately did not disclose he had been present at the post-mortem.

Lara poured two mugs of coffee and slid one in front of Lawson. He noticed she was wearing her Cartier watch.

"That is an impressive, and might I say expensive, looking timepiece. My girlfriend would be very envious if she saw that."

Lara turned her wrist to look at it.

"It was a surprise birthday present from James."

Lawson held his mug with both hands and took a sip.

"So, he chose it without you?"

"Yes. He had good taste and knew what I liked."

The lady was telling an untruth! But so was Lawson as he did not have a girlfriend. What other lies would she tell and why? He was about to find out.

"How often do you cycle into the village?" he asked.

"Most days to collect fresh food. In Poland, we only had fresh produce and that is the way I like to eat it in England, not from a fridge."

"Cycling must keep you fit. Can you drive a car?"

"No" was her short response.

Lara smiled and stood up.

"Would you like to see how I keep fit?" She walked towards a set of open inner doors and into an oak framed glass conservatory. Lawson followed. Before him was a swimming pool with a multi gym and sauna at the far end.

"This is how I relax and keep fit."

Lawson was impressed, but he was there to "flush out" whatever the lady was hiding.

"So being brutally practical. Now that James is dead, who will inherit this house?"

Lara shrugged her shoulders but did not reply.

"Is there a Will?"

"Don't know."

"Did James own the house?"

"I assume so. He never discussed it."

"Have you consulted a solicitor to protect your interests?"

"No."

They walked back into the kitchen and sat down. She poured more coffee. He had endeavoured to sow doubts in her mind, but she still did not seem concerned. It was though, she knew what was going to happen and was waiting for it to happen, but what was it?

Lawson rested his elbows on the worktop and looked directly at her.

"Lara, I want to help. I think you need help."

He paused before continuing.

"I understand you grew up in a small village near Kalisz city in central Poland. It must have been hard not having contact with your family for eight years. How about me, through the British Embassy, contacting them on your behalf?"

The colour drained from her cheeks. She did not reply. Lawson played the game. He showed no emotion. He just sat with elbows forward looking directly at her.

"What's the problem?"

Lara shook her head several times but said nothing.

Who was this man? Did he know she was not Lara Zamoyski or was he just a normal local policeman trying to be kind? How should she respond?

After several minutes of silence, she sat back and smiled.

"Forgive me. My family disowned me years before I came to England. No one must contact them."

Lawson smiled gently.

"You have my promise."

Lara questioned, "I never told you where I lived."

"It's on your UK visa application. Press a button and the information appears on the screen. It is called the wonders of modern science. A computer, you should buy yourself one."

He smiled. It was a deliberate tease to reduce the tension.

Should he push her further? Should he declare his hand? Not yet. Give her the freedom to run but not escape. The secret of a successful interrogation is that the subject does not realise she is being interrogated.

"Have you ever thought about owning a dog? They can be great company."

He opened his wallet and handed her a photograph.

"My Jack Russell."

She held the photograph for a moment and handed it back.

"No thanks, too much responsibility."

Lawson carefully tucked it into his jacket top pocket. He finished his coffee and checked his watch.

"Lara, I must be going. May I contact you again in a few days just to check on your wellbeing?"

"Yes, of course."

She walked with him to the front door and waved goodbye: reassured he was just a policeman trying to be kind. He did not know her secret.

Back in his car, he took the photograph from his top pocket and placed it into an envelope. He had surreptitiously obtained Lara's fingerprints. He did not own a dog. Lawson drove off leaving Special Operations to covertly monitor her response to his visit.

She returned to the kitchen to prepare a salad lunch before spending the afternoon reading and listening to music.

Lara made one telephone call that afternoon. She called the local Mercedes dealership to arrange with them to buy back 'her' car: The recent death of her husband having 'temporarily' left her with a cash-flow problem. Until his estate was sorted out, she needed money urgently for funeral expenses. That was a further untruth!

Early next morning, the coroner's officer called at the house to deliver the clothing and jewellery of the deceased.

He also explained to Lara the process of the forthcoming inquest and the requirement for her, as his next of kin, to formally register the death. The officer's visit was undertaken with the approval of Lawson.

Following the visit, Lara continued in her daily routine and cycled to the general store in the village. Her movements were monitored.

After lunch, she cycled to the railway station at the nearby market town of Pulborough. There she caught a train to Horsham to visit the district council office to register the death of her 'late husband'.

Next, she visited a local jewellers' shop to sell his Rolex watch and jewellery. Again, giving the reason of needing money to cover funeral expenses. As means of authenticating her story, she produced the recently acquired documentation form registering his death. She received a cheque for eight thousand pounds.

Before leaving the town, Lara visited a travel agency to purchase a one-way air flight to Cyprus, scheduled to depart Gatwick Airport three days hence.

Arriving back at Pulborough, she visited her bank. For eight years she had been regarded as a respected customer, residing in one of the more expensive houses in the area. So, when she paid in the two cheques from the sale of the car and jewellery with the heart wrenching story that, on a 'temporary basis', she needed to withdraw most of her savings to cover 'delicate' debts of her 'late husband', the bank obliged. It was agreed she would collect the cash in three days' time.

Back at their office, Lawson and Holloway received a Special Operations email concerning Lara's activities. Holloway commented on the thoroughness of the report, noting the surveillance team had listed each item of food the 'target' had purchased. Much interest was given to the purchasing of an air flight ticket to Cyprus and her visit to the bank.

The last paragraph of the report was by far the most interesting. On arriving back home, Lara had opened the wall combination safe in the study: the safe in which Special Operations had found a large amount of cash, the deeds to the house and her Polish passport. During the first visit made by Lawson and Holloway, she had denied having access to the safe or of knowing what it contained.

Lawson opened his case file and viewed the photograph of Lara's passport taken by Special Operations during the covert search.

"It is still current with almost a year to run. The lady is planning to leave us! She has clearly decided not to wait for the forensic results or the funeral. Nor contest ownership of the house."

He briefed Jane Rigby on the recent developments and was granted authority for the surveillance operation to continue.

Meanwhile, further information was received from colleagues in Poland: Twenty-eight-year-old Lara Zamoyski was unmarried and a fully qualified teacher at a state-run junior school in Kalisz, central Poland. A photograph of the real Lara was enclosed.

Chapter Thirteen

The Game Is Up

Next morning, Lawson made an unannounced solo visit to Timberland Lodge. Lara was as well-groomed and relaxed as ever. She invited him into the kitchen and prepared coffee, making no attempt to ask him the reason for the visit.

"Where is the Mercedes?" He asked with apparent innocence. "I noticed it wasn't parked on the driveway."

"I sold it back to the Mercedes people. No point in me keeping it as I don't drive."

"I understand the post-mortem toxicology results will take a couple of weeks. So, what are your plans for the future?" asked Lawson.

Lara handed him a mug of coffee and sat down opposite.

"That's difficult. Eight years spent in a 'marriage' of convenience without a loving relationship. It is every girl's dream to find that special man. Perhaps, one day." She paused, smiled and with a hint of flirtation in her voice moved closer, "Any suggestions?"

"You are a very attractive woman, and I am sure you will have no problem." He cut short his response, quickly reminding himself he was the hunter and she was his target.

Plus, the sobering thought that his every word was being monitored by Special Operations.

From his wallet he took out a photograph and handed it to her.

"This is my girlfriend. We have been together for over three years."

Lara held it with both hands,

"She is a very pretty girl."

Lawson took the photograph and replaced in his wallet, whilst watching for her reaction. There was none. There was no indication she had recognised the woman in the photograph. It was of the genuine Lara Zamoyski. He doubted the woman sitting opposite him had ever been to Kalisz and was probably not Polish.

"What are you thinking?" He asked.

"Just that she is a lucky girl."

Lawson finished his coffee and smiled.

"This was only a brief visit to check that my favourite lady in Fittleworth was taking care of herself. I sense you may not be as happy as you first appear. Is there anything you wish to discuss or ask me?"

Lara touched him gently on his arm.

"Thank you for your concern. It has been a difficult week. In truth, I am lonely and a little frightened." She shook her head but said nothing more.

Lawson held her lightly with both hands.

"When you are ready, we can have that long talk."

She nodded.

He said goodbye and left the house.

As he walked across the driveway, he noted torn pages from books scattered in an open waste bin. He took a closer glance and was able to identify they were from Jane Austen books. The earlier Special Operations search of the house had identified Jane Austen books in Lara's room. Why had she torn them up and thrown them away?

The surveillance operation continued. No telephone calls were made from or to the house and no one visited. On days two and three, Lara undertook her daily cycle ride to the village general store.

At lunchtime on the third day, she telephoned for a taxi to take her to Pulborough. Following the telephone call, Special Operations monitored her opening the wall safe and removing her passport and the one hundred and fifty thousand pounds. Shortly after, carrying a leather travel bag, she departed in a taxi for Pulborough. The taxi waited for her outside the bank.

In the privacy of a secure room, she was handed over ninety thousand pounds in new fifty-pound Bank of England notes, wrapped in bundles of ten thousand pounds each. Out of view of the staff, she opened her travel bag and took out the covers of a set of Jane Austen books. Between each cover, she placed several bundles of money before returning the 'books' to the bag, which she then secured with a small padlock. In total, the bag now contained over a quarter of a million pound in cash.

The decision was taken to allow her to continue to the airport but intercept her before she boarded the plane. Undertaking surveillance in Cyprus was not considered a practical proposition.

Arriving at Gatwick Airport, Lara checked in for her flight to Arnica International Airport and walked towards the departure lounge. She only had hand luggage. Her travel bag passed through the security scanner without incident. The bag's contents were displayed on the X-ray screen as clothing and a set of books. Looking up at the departure board she noted the flight was on time and departing in two hours. With only a four-and-a-half-hour flight to Cyprus, she would soon be safe. Lara was now feeling relaxed.

She entered the internet café and logged onto a computer to check on Aeroflot flights from Larnaca to Moscow. She also checked the opening times of several local banks in Larnaca. The lady was clearly familiar with using computers and the internet. The surveillance team assessed she was probably intending a short stopover in Cyprus to safely deposit her bag of cash in a local bank before flying on to Moscow. Having completed her internet searches, Lara walked to a more salubrious venue.

Seated in the warmth and comfort of the cocktail bar, she ordered a coffee from the waiter.

From her right, a cup of coffee was placed on the table in front of her. She did not look up, but then became aware that the 'waiter' was moving to sit opposite her. She glanced up. It was Lawson.

He did not speak. He did not smile. He showed no facial expression. He sat with his palms flat together held just below his chin. She did not speak and sat motionless.

Finally, Lawson leaned forward.

"Is it time for our long serious talk?"

Both looked at each other and said nothing.

"You can't leave the UK without a passport."

Lara bit her lip and responded in a hesitant voice.

"I have a passport."

Lawson remained leaning forward and spoke softly.

"But it is not genuine."

133

He placed on the table a photograph.

She looked puzzled before answering.

"That's the photograph of your girlfriend?"

Lawson shook his head slowly.

"No, this is the photograph of Lara Zamoyski, a schoolteacher from Kalisz."

She remained motionless and then spoke in a noticeably quiet voice.

"Who are you?"

"No, the important question is who are you? You are not Lara Zamoyski and I doubt you are even from Poland."

She remained silent.

He leaned across and tapped Lara's travel bag.

"Over a quarter of a million pounds in cash! We do need to talk."

"Are you going to arrest me?" She sounded frightened.

Lawson sat for a moment reflecting on his current role. As a police officer he would be required to arrest people found committing crime and prosecute them according to the law of the land. The function of MI5 was different. It was to ensure the protection of national security by gathering intelligence on hostile activities carried out in the UK. Success was measured on the ability to 'turn' such individuals and not to imprison them. Was she working for a foreign hostile state or for a criminal organisation?

He leaned towards her.

"Your future depends on your full cooperation."

In his mind Lawson pondered the question: *Why was this woman, suspected of involvement with Russian organised crime and a quarter of a million pound in cash, attempting to fly to Cyprus?*

In recent years, the Mediterranean island of Cyprus has witnessed a significant increase in its population with an influx of wealthy individuals, from the former Soviet Union, depositing millions of dollars in cash in what local banks suspect has been a giant scheme to launder the profits of covert Middle east arms sales and the proceeds of Moscow's mafia.

The Russian Central Bank claims the country lost up to twenty-five billion dollars in gold at the time of the coup against Mikhail Gorbachev. In 2011, it was estimated over nineteen billion dollars in deposits were held by banks in Cyprus.

Lawson did not give Lara a choice. He informed her she was being taken into 'safe custody' and would be given an opportunity to explain herself. She was quietly escorted from the airport lounge by two uniformed officers, by-passing normal customs and border control, and placed into a helicopter. Lawson did not travel with her.

Chapter Fourteen
The Interrogation

The Augusta AW169 twin-engine helicopter flew low across Southern England over the rural green countryside of Hampshire and banked steeply towards the coastline, as it descended and landed on the helipad on Saint George's Fort. It is one of the four Victorian sea forts built in the Solent between 1865 and 1880 to provide a defence for Portsmouth Harbour against French invasion. The forts are located about one and a half miles from the Hampshire coast.

The man-made islands are massive concrete structures over two hundred feet across, with an outer skin of granite blocks. The lower foundation walls are sixty feet thick, rising sixty feet from the sea, clad with heavy iron armour plates all round.

The forts consist of two floor levels and a basement. In their day, they housed a detachment of eighty soldiers and were armed with nine thirty-ton guns facing seaward and smaller seven-ton guns to the landward side. During World War II they had anti-aircraft guns. The forts were decommissioned in around nineteen-sixty.

They are now privately owned luxury homes and hospitality centres for high paying guests.

Saint George's Fort is different: It maintains a low profile, purporting to be the private residence of an unnamed wealthy businessman. In reality, it remains government owned and is maintained for use by the UK security services including MI5, MI6, Special Forces and senior military personnel. It is one of the most secure properties in the UK.

Few words were spoken by staff as Lara was escorted from the helicopter and taken down a flight of stairs to the enclosed reception area. Her questions about what was happening went unanswered. Her personal possessions were taken from her and she was taken to a suite of rooms on the lower level.

The accommodation was luxurious: equivalent to a top-class hotel. Initially, she appeared impressed. Again, her attempts to ask questions were ignored. She was simply shown how the facilities worked and left to her own devises. As she walked around the various rooms, she realised all the windows were barred and the only door into the suite had been locked by the staff as they left: she was incarcerated in a luxury prison. All the windows looked out to sea and she had no view of the decking area.

The accommodation was well equipped with expensive toiletries and an extensive library of books, music CDs and selected DVD films, but no newspapers or ability to receive television channels. She was totally isolated from the outside world. No one had given her any indication of the future.

Each mealtime a trolley of excellent food was wheeled in and served by a uniformed waiter. He was polite and professional, referring to her as 'Madam' but did not enter into any conversation. She dined alone. All her actions throughout each day were secretly monitored from behind a two-way mirror.

On the third day, for the first time, the telephone in the lounge area rang. With a sense of relief, she picked up the receiver. It was Lawson. He spoke in a soft friendly fashion and enquired if the accommodation satisfied her needs.

She responded, "Please tell me what is going on" and began to cry.

Lawson, ignored her plea and continued in a caring tone, "Is there anything you would wish me to bring you?"

Lara grasped at the suggestion he might be coming to visit, "When are you coming to see me? Please, please come soon." After a pause she added, "I am so frightened Mr Lawson."

The psychological approach appeared to be working. He rewarded her with some comfort and hope.

"Please call me Julian. I will be flying over to see you in a couple of days. Just hang in there." He then put the phone down.

Lawson turned and faced Jane Rigby, "What a hard-lying bastard have I become." He then turned back and viewed, through the two-way mirror, Lara sitting on the sofa crying.

Together, Lawson and Jane climbed aboard the helicopter and flew back to HQ London.

On day five, he made an early morning visit to the monitoring room at the fort and was given an update on the activity and mental state of Lara. The Watchers considered she was almost ready to talk.

At eight in the morning, the door to Lara's suite was unlocked, opened and a trolley wheeled in.

"Good morning Madam, do you desire a full English breakfast or croissants?"

She began to answer, then stopped and looked up. It was Lawson. Her face lit up as though she had found a long-lost dear friend. He was dressed in a dark blue pin-striped suit and ready to do business.

He smiled, "May I join you for breakfast? I have just flown in from London and thought we might have croissants and coffee together."

She just nodded and looked very relieved.

Lawson laid the table and sat opposite her.

"Let us have a quiet friendly breakfast together, with no nasty talk about that horrible real world out there."

Again, Lara did not immediately respond but simply nodded in agreement and, after a pause added, "Thank you."

He kept the conversation light, appearing friendly and talking about pleasant things in life. In reality, he was very much keeping to his professional role and painting an enticing picture of an idyllic life that might be waiting for her in England. After a leisurely breakfast he agreed to return in an hour to discuss her future, carefully avoiding the question that he would be asking her to tell all.

Lawson climbed the steps to the top level of the fort and, in the morning sunshine, joined Jane for a refreshing cold drink and a chat. They agreed: Lara was now ready to be turned.

Exactly one hour later, he returned. Lara was looking extremely attractive. As he took his seat on the sofa, he complemented her on her choice of dress. Mentally, he reminded himself he was the 'interrogator' and she was the 'villain'. Also, with a secret smile, he reminded himself Jane, his Boss, was watching and listening from behind the two-way mirror.

Lawson beckoned Lara to take the soft armchair facing him. He sat silent for a few seconds, with his hands clasped in front of him and with his chin lightly resting on his index fingers. He then spoke slowly and deliberately.

"Lara, we need to talk. And we need to talk seriously. Some of what I have to say will upset you. It is for your own good. And it is not my intention to hurt you."

He paused and leaned forward.

"I am an MI5 officer. We work on facts, not rumour nor speculation but straight forward facts. I will be truthful with you. All I demand from you is the truth. Sometimes this will be hard." He left a space for her to think and respond.

She sat facing him but starring over his head to the open and barred window and the calm sea beyond.

Lawson did not interrupt her thoughts and sat quietly looking directly into her eyes. After a silence of several minutes, she caught his gaze and responded with a nervous smile.

He learned further forward, almost touching her clasped hands, and continued in a soft, deliberate and slow voice.

"You are not who you say you are. You were travelling on a false passport. You had two hundred and fifty thousand pounds in your possession when attempting to flee the UK. Your late 'husband' was not who you said he was. He was also using a false passport. And I have good reason to believe you lived with several other men, all falsely purporting to be British citizens calling themselves Mr James Whitehead. That is a good few facts to begin with."

Several times Lara opened her mouth and took a deep breath, but no words came out. Lawson considered she was genuinely frightened about the outcome.

Still leaning towards her, he placed his hands over hers and gently gripped them.

"Lara, what you don't know is that the man you refer to as your husband was murdered. He was injected with highly toxic poison which caused him to have a heart attack. Tests on his DNA identify him as being from Eastern Europe. Dentistry on his teeth was most likely undertaken in Russia. Even his wedding ring was produced from Russian gold. A good case to think he was Russian."

Most of what Lawson said appeared not to register with Lara. She concentrated on one fact and enquired, "Are you sure he was murdered?"

Lawson retained holding her hands between his.

"Yes, he was murdered. And there is every chance your life is in mortal danger."

She shook her head, "No, I've done nothing wrong for them to kill me."

He removed his hands from her hands and slowly sat back. He did not speak nor show any emotion, except continue to look into her eyes. He let silence do his work: *Silence being the best interrogator for the truth.*

Lara nervously fluttered her eyes, as it began to dawn on her what she had just said.

Lawson sat for another full minute before leaning forward and quietly repeating Lara's last response, "No, I've done nothing wrong for them to kill me."

Her silence continued. Gently stroking her hands to offer reassurance, he whispered, "Who are they?"

She began to shake her head with eyes closed.

"If I tell you anything then I will be killed."

Lawson reverted to his original position of clasping his hands with his chin resting on his index fingers. "Lara, you have been playing a grown-up and dangerous game. The rules for both sides are clearly defined. If you do not cooperate with us, I can guarantee that you will end up dead."

Lara responded without a pause, "Why? How?"

Lawson showed his ruthless professional side and, without emotion.

"If you choose to cooperate, your reward will be freedom to live a good life in this country financially secure."

He paused and then continued at a slower pace.

"If you do not, you will be of no use to us. We will have no responsibility for your safety. You will be put on a direct flight to Moscow. However, I must warn you about the reception you will receive on arrival. Your 'friends' would ask why you had been set free? They might conclude you had told us everything. That would not make them happy. And, to make sure, we would leak disinformation saying you had talked. Lara, it is a cruel world, but you chose to be a player. Now you alone must decide on your destiny."

He stood up and left the room, locking the door behind him.

She also stood up and shouted.

"You bastard. You English bastard."

He strolled to the top deck and poured himself a coffee, before taking a seat at a table shielding the morning sun with a large umbrella. The decking area had the appearance of a large modern cruise liner. With the fort located in mid-channel, it reminded him of happier days of returning from a cruise with his dear late wife, sailing back up the Solent to the Port of Southampton. He opened his iPod and typed up notes of his meeting with Lara.

Back in her room, Lara picked up the telephone.

"Please ask Mr Lawson to come back. I will join his team."

She did not wait for a reply before replacing the receiver.

Lawson was called to the monitoring room to meet with Jane and Doctor Emanuel Greythorn, the department's resident psychologist. Lara's telephone call was discussed.

The doctor considered her mental state 'fragile and vulnerable' and added that she was a 'born survivor' who had weighed up the situation and decided to cooperate. He commented, "Gently lead her: Don't push. And give her constant reassurance."

Lawson moved closer to Jane and spoke quietly.

"Can I guarantee her immunity from prosecution?"

Jane nodded, "From the top, I have that authority."

Lawson entered Lara's room and sat on the sofa next to her. She appeared more relaxed than the last time he was with her and had regained her composure. She took the initiative.

"You want the truth, and I will give you the truth."

She smiled and continued.

"Please treat me as your equal. We are both professionals at our jobs. You believe you work for the good guys. Once I believed I worked for the good guys."

He responded.

"I always tell the truth."

Before he could continue, Lara interrupted.

"No Julian, you don't. Let me be the 'interrogator' for a minute."

He smiled and gestured.

"Please proceed."

She teased him.

"When we met earlier this morning, you said you had just flown in. That was an untruth. Your suit trousers did not have a single crumpled crease in them. Your freshly polished shoes did not have a single speck of outside dirt on them. I bet you only got dressed ten minutes or so before you came into my room,"

Lara moved closer.

"When you came in, I could smell your hair had been freshly washed. If I am not mistaken, it was the same shampoo fragrance as the shampoo in my bathroom. Supplied to this established courtesy of MI5?"

Lawson was not sure whether to feel impressed or embarrassed.

"May I continue now?" he asked.

She was enjoying teasing him.

"Not quite. Before coming back to see me, you had a briefing in a small closed room with your female chief. I would suggest she is in her mid-forties and an elegant lady with style."

Lawson pulled a quizzical facial expression.

Lara moved even closer and still in teasing mode continued.

"My sensitive nose detects the pleasant aroma of an expensive, yet discrete French perfume. No doubt, that of your boss."

He smiled with a sense of professional appreciation.

"I couldn't possibly comment."

She stood up and with a wry smile said.

"Of course, you can't. The lady is probably listening to every word of our conversation. Julian, I now hand the 'interrogation whip' back to you."

Chapter Fifteen
The Confession

Lawson took a small digital voice recorder from his jacket pocket and placed it on the coffee table. He smiled at Lara.

"Shall we begin?"

He leaned forward and switched on the machine.

Lara sat upright and correct, as though composing herself to appear before a panel at a job interview. She spoke in a calm clear voice and knew what was required:

"My true name is Alexandra Greshneva. I am a citizen of Russia. I was born in the industrial city of Volgograd. It was previously called Stalingrad. You will be aware of the Battle of Stalingrad. It was the longest and most bloody battle of World War II. My grandfather was a resistance fighter in that battle and was killed at the age of just twenty-four. He was posthumously made a Hero of the Soviet Union. Most of his family was also killed during the battle for Stalingrad.

"At the time, my father was three years old. He grew up in great poverty, but with a strong will and was proud to be Russian. After service in the regular army, he joined the KGB and rose to the rank of colonel in the First Chief Directorate (Foreign Operations)."

Lawson interjected.

"That's running espionage operations against foreign powers?"

She nodded and continued.

"In my late teens I became a student at the KGB Krasnoznamennyi Institute. We were the elite. It was a very secretive training school for 'illegals', located in a forest outside Moscow. Most students were the children of KGB officers. It was to be a three-year course. We were taught every requirement needed of an agent to live under deep cover in a foreign country. One of the requirements was to learn a foreign language fluently. I studied English."

Lawson poured out a fresh coffee and handed it to her.

"I gather the World changed before you graduated?"

She took the coffee cup and held it in her hands, before giving a faint smile.

"I'd been at the institute for a year when the Soviet Union collapsed and dissolved into fifteen independent states. With this came the dissolution of the KGB. Thousands of officers and agents became unemployed. Many quickly saw ways to use their talents elsewhere: Some took up high level Government positions and some, by dubious means, became billionaires almost overnight. Many involved themselves in major criminal activity."

Lawson asked, "What was your take on all this?"

She was pensive and looked directly into his eyes.

"Julian, the certainties suddenly disappeared. Like my dear father, I was proud of my country and proud to be a young member of the KGB: The service protected the country from outside aggressors and internal agitators. As I said to you earlier today, I believed we were the good guys."

Lawson said, "Before we continue, may I still call you Lara?"

"Yes, of course. It's the name I feel comfortable with."

He continued, "Earlier today you actually said, 'Once I believed I worked for the good guys.' Does this infer your view changed after the fall of the Soviet Union?"

Lara nodded her head.

"Yes, my eyes were opened to greed, violence and crime. It was all taking place in the chaos of the country I loved and admired. I was now unemployed, with no money and little prospect of an honest living. Slowly I became part of a criminal organisation run by senior ex-KGB officers."

Lawson suggested, "Can you give me an overview of the organisation?"

She responded, "From the outset, it was set up and run by ex-KGB. By its very nature, it was secretive and organised on KGB principles: You are only told what you need to know, and you never ask questions nor disclose what you know. It has tentacles everywhere and into everything. I know very few names. The ones I do know are probably false."

He interrupted her flow.

"OK, let us take it step by step. You first came to England about eight years ago. How was that arranged and for what purpose?"

Lara replied, "For several years life had been difficult. Then a KGB acquaintance of my father invited me to Cyprus for a free holiday with the promise of some paid work. After the first week, I was offered the chance of working in England as a housekeeper, which brought with it accommodation and a regular wage. Only after I accepted, was I given the false passport and told that I must pose as that Polish girl. The reason given seemed plausible: As a Russian I would not get a work visa. However, by posing as a Polish national, it being part of the European Union, I could enter this country without any restrictions."

Lawson asked, "So how did you get to England?"

Lara replied, "The man in Cyprus gave me the passport, an air ticket and a mobile telephone number I was to phone when I arrived at Heathrow Airport."

In response to a series of questions, Lara gave an account of her first month in Britain:

She arrived at Heathrow Airport on a cold wet dark winters evening and telephoned the number she had been given. A man came and collected me. From the outset, she took an instant dislike of him. His initial action was to ask for her passport, which he scrutinised with great care: Very reminiscent of a Soviet border check.

He was in his fifties, short with a muscular upper body and a shaven head. He wore a long black leather jacket and dirty creased trousers. She thought of him as an old angry Russian bear: a man not to be crossed.

The man gave his name as 'Mr Green' but did not enter into a conversation. He had an English name but clearly was not English. She thought he was most likely to have been ex-KGB: probably recruited from the lower ranks of the army and used as an 'enforcer'. She acknowledged such men existed in the time of the Soviet Union.

The Enforcer drove a modern silver Mercedes car which, Lara considered, was 'unloved' and had never been cleaned. The exterior was heavily mud splattered and the interior was even worse. It smelled of the man's stale body odour and cigarette smoke. They drove for about thirty minutes to a house situated in a quiet residential suburb on the outskirts of London.

It was a large five-bedroom nineteen-thirties style house, with a minimal amount of furniture and a very unkempt front garden. She assumed the place had been rented. Like the car, it was certainly unloved. She was never told the address. The man's body odour and cigarette smoke pervaded throughout the house. It was a cold and unfriendly place to live.

The man remained uncommunicative and busied himself in things she did not understand. She was told her responsibilities were to clean the house and undertake the cooking. Throughout the following days other men, of a similar description and attitude to the Enforcer, came and went but never spoke to her. She wondered if it was a cheap lodging house for Eastern European workers passing through.

Lara was not allowed out on her own. When she protested, the Enforcer threatened her and said if she made a fuss, he would kick her out and tell the police she was an illegal immigrant with false papers. This frightened her.

At the beginning of the second week, the Enforcer took her on a day trip to Central London. He remained a man of few words but was not quite so frightening. It was clearly intended as a day out to buy her expensive things and impress her. She was not sure why, but it had the desired effect. It was a different world: She was taken aback by the riches of Mayfair, with its palatial houses and luxury cars parked in every street.

He took her to Harrods and other top establishments and, allowed her to purchase expensive clothes and designer handbags and shoes. Money appeared in abundant supply. Payment was always in cash. She was smitten by the luxury and pleasure the lifestyle could bring: She had been drawn into the web, but she remained unsure what it was all about.

Over the following days, the Enforcer remained just as mysterious, and she certainly would not wish to upset him. On one occasion, she had inadvertently caught a glimpse of him in the bathroom with his jacket off, and noticed he was wearing a shoulder holster. Although only a momently glance, her KGB training enabled her to identify he was carrying a Russian made semi-automatic pistol.

Lara was given an additional task. The Enforcer explained that from the house a website agency was being run: An agency to supply beautiful young Russian brides to middle-aged lonely British men. Her job was to vet the application forms.

The agency was only interested in accepting men aged about forty years and having a UK passport, British driver's licence and a national insurance number. Plus, they must be single and have no police criminal conviction or appear on a debt agency register. This was explained away by saying the agency must protect the prospective brides, by ensuring the men were genuine upright citizens of the UK.

Some of the other requirements puzzled Lara: Why did successful applicants have to live in the northern part of the country and not own their own house nor have any living relatives or close friends? The last two points would be discreetly ascertained when they reached the interview stage. Lara had been raised in an environment where one did not ask questions, and, in fact, it would have been dangerous to do so.

At the end of the fourth week of her stay, the Enforcer asked Lara to accompany him to Heathrow Airport. En-route, they stopped at a small shabby looking hotel and picked up a man carrying a single suitcase. He appeared excited at the prospect of travelling abroad. Few words were spoken during the car journey but, in his excitement, Lara was able to elicit he was flying to Moscow to meet his future Russian bride. She also heard the Enforcer getting confirmation from the man that he had not told anyone about his planned trip: As the UK government did not approve of the practice.

On reaching passport control, the enforcer handed the man his travelling documents. Lara noted his name was Mr James Whitehead. He rushed through Customs without a backwards glance.

Back at the house, the administration work Lara had been doing for the Russian bride agency ceased. From that moment forward, she was only required to undertake cleaning and cooking duties. She still was not permitted to leave the house unescorted. All trace of the agency existence just vanished from the house. No explanation was given. It was as though the agency had functioned to find only one applicant.

Two weeks passed when, again, the Enforcer asked Lara to accompany him to Heathrow Airport. No explanation was given. They did not stop to pick up anyone. Having parked his Mercedes in the multi-storey car park, they walked to the Arrival Lounge.

After a wait of thirty minutes, and from the crowd of arriving passengers, a man walked across to them and shook the Enforcer's hand. Lara had never seen him before and gained the impression, the Enforcer and the stranger had not previously met. However, in the crowded terminal, they had been able to identify each other. She assumed the stranger must be ex-KGB, with a pre-arranged signal having been used.

The stranger had about him an air of arrogant authority. He handed Lara his suitcase to carry as he indulged in quietly spoken conversation with the Enforcer. She assumed the new man was way up the pecking order from the lowly bullying Enforcer. As they walked back to the car, Lara looked down at the travel label attached to the suitcase. It read: Mr James WHITEHEAD. This was certainly not the shy lonely Mr James WHITEHEAD they had seen off two weeks earlier so eager to collect his new Russian bride.

Lawson looked towards Lara, smiled and turned the voice recorder off. "We have been talking for over two hours I suggest we take a break and lunch."

Lara returned the smile and nodded.

Chapter Sixteen
The Arrival of Mr Whitehead

It was the first time in five days since Lara had seen outside the confines of her suite. Lawson guided her to the top deck of the fort and to a table set aside from the others. It was shielded on three sides with glass partitions and large exotic plants. They were served a three-course meal with wine. Lara noted that, apart from the waiter, no other people were present in the vicinity. She considered this a deliberate act: The lady was being rewarded for her cooperation, but not yet trusted to be with other members of the department.

After a leisurely lunch, coffee was served. They turned their chairs to look out over the Solent and engaged in further conversation. It was early September: One of the last warm days of summer with a refreshing gentle breeze flowing across the sea. The view was spectacular. Pleasure yachts were sailing nearby and passenger ferries crossing in both directions from the mainland to the Isle of Wight.

Lara thought Lawson had a pleasant easy manner but was aware he never let down his guard. She still knew nothing about him or his private life. However, she was beginning to feel comfortable and safe in his presence.

In a soft voice she asked, "Are you married?"

"Widowed" was his one-word reply.

"Sorry," and after a hesitant pause, "Would you care to talk about it?"

He was not annoyed but chose not to respond to her request.

"Lara, we had better get back. I would like another two hours before calling it a day."

They returned to her suite. Lawson turned on the voice recorder.

"We adjourned at the point the new Mr Whitehead arrived. Please continue from there."

Lara sat back in her chair and continued with her recollection of events.

"I was beginning to feel uneasy. I was not naïve; after all I had trained with the KGB."

Lawson interrupted her flow.

"Correction, you were a full member of the KGB."

She grinned, "Yes, a full member."

"Please continue."

"Having been a member of the KGB, I was aware that people taken into their care did disappear. It was now evident I was involved with a criminal organisation. It did not take a genius to work out, that the Russian bride agency had been set up for the sole purpose of luring one suitable and unfortunate man into the net. I had no illusions: the genuine James Whitehead had been killed to facilitate their plan. The 'new' Mr Whitehead would now have his identity tailored to meet the needs of the UK operation."

With further questions, and gentle prompting, Lawson gained the story from Lara:

This form of penetration into a hostile country had been a specialty of the KGB. "Illegals" (illegal spies) were placed to gain political, economic and military secrets and, sometimes, disinformation to discredit that country's government. Now, the same skills were being deployed for organised crime. For what purpose, Lara did not know. However, there was no doubt that the new Mr Whitehead was an ex-KGB senior officer.

Back at the London house, Mr Whitehead remained aloof. For two days he engaged in intense discussions with the Enforcer. On occasions, Lara heard the two men speaking in Russian. Unknown men also visited the house and met with Mr Whitehead. When speaking in English, he had the accent, mannerisms and clothing, of a typical English gentleman. Lara considered he had been well trained. He was in complete contrast to the unsophisticated Enforcer.

On the third day of his stay, Mr Whitehead had called Lara to his room. No one else was present. He spoke in Russian. He was well educated and spoke with cold ruthless authority. She was not able to ask questions: Just to listen and obey. He told her only what she needed to know and no more: Tomorrow they would travel to West Sussex to view a large country house, which he intended to purchase and live in.

She would be introduced as his wife. In the future, she would be expected to deal with the local tradesmen and officials. In practice, they would not be married. He would not expect any sexual relationship with her. Lara would have her separate bedroom and would function as the housekeeper, with responsibility for the house budget. He would often be away from the house. She would simply tell people her "husband" was a busy businessman travelling abroad. He would avoid any contact with local people. She would live in luxury and receive more money than she had ever had before.

Lara was not asked if she agreed: She was simply receiving her instructions. Lara had no choice in the matter. She knew what the consequences would be if she refused.

Early the next morning, wearing her recently purchased expensive dress and shoes; she had left the house with Mr Whitehead. He drove the silver Mercedes previously used by the Enforcer. However, it had been valeted inside and out. It looked and smelled as though it had just left the car showroom. During the journey he spoke little but handed her a gold wedding ring and a large diamond ring to wear.

Arriving at the house in West Sussex, she was impressed. It was Timberland Lodge, the country house she had subsequently lived in until a few days earlier. They were met by the estate agent and a local solicitor, who had been instructed to act for Mr Whitehead. After a brief tour of the house, he said he would buy it.

He told the two men he would often be away on business and his wife (Lara) had the authority to act on his behalf in all matters: She would sign all the documents. Purchase of the house would be a cash deal. He insisted on the transaction to be completed within seven days, when he and his wife would move in. With the deal done, Mr and Mrs Whitehead drove away leaving the two men to finalise the paperwork.

Seven days later, they moved into the house. Lara had access to the 'house' bank account and dealt with all matters. Mr Whitehead's signature did not appear on any document. In the coming year, Mr Whitehead would frequently be away for many days at a time. She never asked what he did, and he never explained anything. The local tradesmen and people in the nearby village knew her as Mrs Whitehead. Mr Whitehead was rarely at home and never met any of the locals.

Lawson interrupted at this point.

"Didn't you find this set up rather strange?"

Lara laughed. It was the first time he had heard her laugh.

"Strange, from an Englishman's perspective perhaps. Remember, back at the KGB institute I was being trained for an undercover existence. Then it was for the State. Now I was doing it for an organisation, which was being run on KGB lines by ex-KGB officers. The main difference was I never expected to be living in such luxury."

She then continued by explaining the strict set of rules against which she operated: Maintain cover story at all times; must not develop any friendship with local people; must not invite anyone back to the house; must not telephone nor communicate in any way with friends or family.

Once a year, she was permitted to fly to Cyprus for two weeks holiday, staying at a small hotel owned by a former KGB colleague. This was the only place she was authorised to stay. Lara had known the owner since her childhood. He had been a colonel in the KGB, working alongside her father in the First Chief Directorate (Foreign Operations). She believed he knew about her role in the UK, and likely to have been active in the organisation, but he never mentioned it. He would simply enquire if she were happy living in the UK.

She would travel to Cyprus using the passport by the name Lara Zamoyski. She would meet with old KGB acquaintances, but was only permitted to say she was living in the UK. She was forbidden to make any mention of Mr Whitehead or the house.

Lara sensed some, possibly many, of the acquaintances were undoubtedly involved in major criminal activity but this was never discussed: That was the KGB way. Lara never had 'friends' in the KGB, only 'colleagues' and "acquaintances."

Lawson asked her how she viewed the setup in Cyprus.

She replied, "I regarded Cyprus as the Post Box for the wider tentacles of the various Russian criminal organisations. It exists to facilitate operations abroad."

"And what would that include?" asked Lawson.

Lara was hesitant, taking time to compose her reply.

"Anything that was requested: Assassination; gathering evidence or tracking down dissidents or oligarchs who were critics of Russia; protection rackets; buying properties and weapons running."

Lawson leaned forward and spoke quietly.

"Who were the customers?"

Lara replied in a quiet voice, as if mimicking him.

"Sometimes criminal organisations; sometimes the State and sometimes no one knew. That is the sort of world we had become."

The nuances of her last comment were not lost on Lawson: activities could be undertaken on behalf of criminal organisations or the State – and sometimes the nature of the 'client' remained unknown.

Lara continued that after a year, Mr Whitehead informed her that he would be departing, but did not say where to, and that a new Mr James Whitehead would take his place. There was no further explanation. The new man arrived almost immediately, and matters continued as before.

Lawson sat back incredulous, shaking his head.

"How on earth could you work in such an environment?"

"Simple. I was the housekeeper of a large house and, occasionally, the tenant changed."

Lawson enquired, "So how many Mr Whiteheads came and went?"

She replied, "Six."

"And did the format remain the same?"

"Exactly. Some were more polite than others, but the rules remained the same."

Lawson asked, "I am unclear on how you received further instructions."

She replied, "This was a 'deep-cover' operation. Everything was correctly set up at the outset. It functioned without the danger of further communication between the Centre and their operatives. Remember, it was run like a KGB long-term operation by ex-KGB. I was low in their pecking order. I was the paid servant facilitating 'base-camp' for the important people. All I needed to maintain the 'base-camp' was a monthly income, and this was supplied by the man calling himself Mr Whitehead."

Lawson relaxed his posture and looked directly into her eyes.

"Lara, it has not escaped the attention of my department that, when living in West Sussex, you seem to always buy the Wednesday edition of the Telegraph, but not on other days. I have a possible explanation, but would you care to enlighten me?"

She looked as though she had been caught out.

"Ah, yes. The alert procedure. An item would appear in the personal column of the Wednesday edition of the Daily Telegraph. It would simple read: Jonathan FA. Please make contact. Jane FA."

Lawson asked, "What did it mean?"

Lara remained looking guilty.

"For me to expect the arrival of a new Mr Whitehead within the next few days."

"And how did this take place?"

"He would arrive in a taxi. I would show him around the house. The house and car keys would be on the desk in the study, having been left there by the previous Mr Whitehead. To repeat myself: I was the housekeeper and I was meeting the new tenant."

Lawson asked, "What would you say were the common characteristics, the six Mr Whitehead's shared?"

Lara replied, "That is an easy one to answer. I have no doubt they were all highly trained ex-KGB. All were in excellent physical and mental shape: at their operational peak. They were men who would not be intimidated but would cause severe problems to people who crossed them."

Lawson continued.

"Were you ever told, or did you ever suspect, what one or more of the Mr Whiteheads' had been involved in?"

Lara nodded.

"None told me anything about their work. However, about two years ago I watched a TV news report about the death of a Russian billionaire living in this country. He had apparently died whilst out jogging. I thought to myself it had the hallmarks of a KGB hit. A couple of days later, the then Mr Whitehead arrived back at the house and seemed happy. He made a brief comment about having had a successful business trip. This was unusual. I had never seen him smile or make such a comment to me. Then, without further explanation he referred to me as 'Mrs Whitehead' and invited me for a day out in London. Again, this was totally out of character. We had a pleasant day together and visited top class jewellers in Bond Street, where he bought himself and me expensive watches."

Lawson stopped her in mid-flow.

"Was that the Cartier watch we discussed back at your house when you, incorrectly, told me 'Mr Whitehouse' had bought it for you as a surprise present?"

Lara replied, "Yes."

She continued.

"He then wined and dined me at an expensive restaurant, and we had a good time. Next day he was gone: Without saying goodbye or explanation."

Lawson was interested in this last revelation.

"Which number Mr Whitehead was this one?"

"Number five. The last but one."

Lawson added, "We actually have a CCTV recording of you both in a jewellers' shop in New Bond Street, purchasing the watch. It then shows you both driving away in a blue Audi A3"

Lara confirmed the fact.

He then said, "And you were driving the car. At an earlier meeting you told me you couldn't drive."

She shrugged her shoulders.

"Sorry, that was a little lie."

Lawson asked, "Am I correct in saying you do not hold a British Driving Licence?"

"Yes."

"But you still drive?"

"Occasionally, if there is a need."

Lara sensed Lawson's train of thought.

"Julian, have you ever seen a policeman stop a new luxury car being driven by an expensively dressed lady? Never."

She explained that it suited her cover story to appear not to be able to drive a car.

Lawson continued with his questions.

"Did you have sex with him? I am thinking: is that why he bought you expensive jewellery and wined and dined you?"

Lara was annoyed by his remark.

"No. I sensed he was happy with his 'success' and wanted to celebrate. Success in our game usually means a big cash reward."

Lawson asked another impertinent question.

"Did you ever have sex with any of the Mr Whiteheads?"

She continued to look annoyed, but then smiled.

"Just one. The last Mr Whitehead."

Lawson, sensing her annoyance, apologised for his intrusion and then continued with his line of questioning.

"Why him?"

"He was a little different from the others. Just as professional, but slightly more human in his outlook. A few times, in the last two months, he brought home small presents, such as chocolates, and occasionally asked after my well-being. He told me he was coming to the end of his stay. Something the others had never mentioned. Yes, I had sex with him and enjoyed it."

"What were your feelings towards him?" asked Lawson.

Lara replied, "In the last two months I began to feel genuine affection for him. I was a little lonely and he felt the need of a woman. Please can we stop for the day?"

Lawson replied, "Just a few more questions, then we will adjourn. Is it possible that the organisation became aware of the friendship? If the friendship had developed it would have ruined the UK operation. Was he poisoned by his own side?"

Lara shook her head.

"Possible, but unlikely. The affection was behind closed doors. He was professional at his job and would never have disclosed, nor hinted, the fact to anyone. And I certainly did not."

Lawson referred to his small leather-bound notebook.

"You say there were six Mr Whiteheads in the eight-year period. Did they all stay for the same length of time?"

"No. In each case it was different. The shortest was just two months and the longest about eighteen months."

"So, there were periods when no Mr Whitehead was in residence?"

Lara shook her head in agreement.

"Yes, often. Sometimes I would not see a Mr Whitehead for two or three months."

Lawson asked, "Why the disparity in the time each one stayed?"

"I assume each came for a specific mission and when that was accomplished, they returned to base."

He continued with this theme.

"You have acknowledged visiting London with Mr Whitehead number five. Please explain other visits you may have had with the others."

Lara was looking tired but continued.

"When you spoke with me back at the house, I explained how the late Mr Whitehead would take me to London a couple of times each year but didn't mix with other people. That was, and remains, a correct statement. Except, it applied collectively to several of the Mr Whiteheads. They were all cultured Russians and enjoyed the arts. Occasionally, we would attend concerts and ballet performances in London."

Lara had clearly had enough. Her mental state was fragile, push her further and she may well close into her shell and so Lawson brought the session to a close. He appeared in a thoughtful business mood. He thanked Lara for her cooperation and left her suite, locking the door behind him. Lawson reported back to Jane on the outcome of the meeting.

Later that evening he met with Jane Rigby and the team, to review what had been achieved and to consider future action. What Lara had said so far had a degree of authenticity and matched with what the department knew about recent criminal and State sponsored operations, emanating from Russia. Much more was required from Lara: the gentle interrogation would continue in the morning.

Lara was served with an 8 am breakfast after which Lawson entered her room to continue with the interrogation, although he preferred to call it a meeting. Now she was cooperating, he decided to adopt a slightly more relaxed approach. Gone was his formal pin-striped suit of previous meetings, replaced by smart casual clothing.

"Lara, for the moment, lets concentrate on talking about the last Mr Whitehead. I am particularly interested in your personal relationship with him and why this may have contributed to him being murdered and by whom. You clearly developed a liking for each other which culminated in a sexual relationship. I have a strong sense that you discussed a possible future together and he probably, my assumption, gave you a good indication why he was in the UK. What did he tell you?"

Silence. Lara endeavoured to avoid direct eye contact and nervously fiddled with a ring on her left middle finger. Still not making eye contact, she slowly shook her head as if arguing with her inner self over what response she should give.

Lawson gently interjected: "It's difficult, but you must tell me. Without it we cannot help or protect you."

Lara speaking slowly, and being deliberately careful with her words, began to explain: "I don't know the details. He did not want me to know the full facts, because he feared it would put my life at risk if things went wrong. Like the others before him, he was here to undertake an assassination of a Russian in this country: a billionaire oligarch, who had fled our motherland when he fell out with formal colleagues within President Putin's government."

"Do you know the name of the target?"

"No, but he had a large house somewhere in Mayfair and was involved in banking and property deals. My Mr Whitehead spent some weeks undertaking surveillance on him and had acquired a detailed knowledge of his daily routine. His house was in a gated community with top-class security. The man had two full-time bodyguards whenever he left his house. They were both Russian and each carried a concealed handgun which, I assume, is illegal in the UK. They drove him around in an armoured Mercedes which contained more powerful automatic guns concealed in the car."

Lawson asked: "Are you aware of any plans, photographs or documents Mr Whitehead had following his surveillance?"

"No, he was a professional and would never keep such things. It would all be stored in his head."

"An assassin will look for a weak point in a targets protection cover. Did Mr Whitehead find one?" enquired Lawson.

"Yes. The target was very fond of his two young daughters. Each Sunday he would take them out to a small quiet country restaurant for lunch. The two bodyguards would remain nearby in the car. After lunch, the children would pester their father to take them out into the rear secluded restaurant garden to play on the swings. Mr Whitehead established he could access the garden via the nearby woodland. He satisfied himself by using the cover of the woods he could undertake the assassination, with a high-powered rifle, and safely make his escape before the bodyguards had time to react."

"Not very subtle" commented Lawson "And clearly a killing that would generate much press interest and speculation."

Lara smiled. "Some assassinations are never identified as such and are recorded as accidents, suicides or death from natural causes. And the 'clients' are happy with that. However, on occasions the clients, especially when State sponsored, are more than happy for a death to be seen as an assassination. It sends a message to other defectors: wherever you hide we will find and eliminate you."

Lawson was aware that in Russia, defectors are regarded as traitors not to be tolerated or ever forgiven. They will be sought out wherever they go and can never drop their guard. A reported brutal death will act as a deterrent to others and indicate to other countries that there will be consequences if they give a safe haven to such people.

"So, what prevented the assassination taking place?" asked Lawson.

Lara continued: "The children. The target seemed so happy and relaxed with his children. Mr Whitehead had previously seen active service with the KGB's elite commando unit in Afghanistan and killed many people in bloody circumstances. I feel he had just reached a stage where he'd had enough of death and wanted out. So, he confided his concerns and thoughts with me."

"Were his sponsors aware of his feelings?"

"Yes. The agreed date for the assassination came and went with nothing happening. Questions were being asked and he had agreed to meet with someone, I don't know who or where, but he was afraid."

Lawson pondered: "So Mr Whitehead is carefully assassinated, with the sponsors hoping it will be seen as a heart attack. And within hours, no doubt, the assassin is safely out of the country. Did he tell you anything about what the other Mr Whiteheads got up too?"

"No, but from what he said I'm now sure each came to the UK to undertake an assassination on behalf of a criminal enterprise or the State."

Lawson added: "As a fully trained agent, let's be honest, at an early stage of your time in this country, you must have had a good idea what this whole enterprise was about: tracking down Russian citizens who had fled their country and their liquidation on behalf of criminal or State sponsors."

No reply was necessary. Lara simply nodded in agreement.

"With Mr Whitehead's change of heart, did he have contact with or seek protection from a UK 'friendly' security service. MI6 perhaps?"

"He did mention the possibility, but I'm not aware he did so."

"Let us consider your future. You were intending to fly to Cyprus with a lot of money. What were your plans beyond, let us say, next week?"

Lara looked drained both mentally and physically. "Beyond next week! Even that seemed a long time in the future. Everything has happened so unexpectedly. I was suddenly alone. I felt in danger in this country and just needed to get out. In Cyprus I felt I had friends but…" She stopped in mid-sentence.

"But, your friends in Cyprus are also 'friends' of the criminal gangs and the State. If they have to choose—" Lawson didn't finish the sentence, but simply gestured with his hands open.

Lara understood the danger she would be in if she travelled to Cyprus or, for that matter, any part of the World. "I will always be in danger and eventually they would find me."

Lawson reported back to Jane and the team. What Lara had told him seemed genuine. However, it would require much further research to identify other players still active in the UK. Plus, possible victims whose deaths may have been incorrectly recorded as death by natural causes or suicide.

Clearly, the long-term operation run from Timberland Lodge had been compromised. Therefore, MI5 could not consider attempting to run with it to uncover future intelligence. Likewise, the service could not support an operation to allow Lara to travel to Cyprus.

Lawson commented, "The two most pressing issues for consideration: Did Mr Whitehead have dealings with our sister service MI6 and what do we do with Lara?"

Jane reported that she had already spoken with MI6 and they denied any knowledge of Mr Whitehead or of the activities carried out at Timberland Lodge. She added, with an element of sarcasm, in her voice: "They would say that, wouldn't they."

The team spent another night at the Fort. Next morning, at 6:15 am there was a knock at Lawson's bedroom door. He checked his watch before opening the door. "Morning sir, Jane Rigby requires you and the team to report to the conference room in fifteen minutes."

Lawson entered the conference room. Jane was already seated and speaking on the telephone to London HQ. She concluded her phone call and looked up: "Lara is dead."

Lawson and the other members, who had heard the pronouncement as they entered the room, sat in silence around the table.

Jane continued: "At six o'clock a member of staff took Lara her normal early morning cup of tea and found her dead with a dressing-gown cord around her neck. The on-duty doctor attended but there was nothing he could do. She had been dead for several hours."

Looking towards Lawson she added: "Please ensure your written record of interrogation is up-to-date. She was a professional agent. She knew the risks and there was no way out of her predicament. There will be no publicity. HQ will deal with the matter. This was a successful operation. Let us pack our bags and be out of here by 9 am"

The words and assessment were given without emotion. Lawson thought to himself: what a hard bastard.

This was a case with lines of investigations still to be undertaken and important questions still to be answered. Back at London HQ Lawson urged Jane Rigby to lobby for the case to remain active. She refused to discuss the issue. The matter was politically sensitive and no further investigation would be undertaken. The file was closed. The direction had come from the top. The reasons would not be disclosed.

Lawson felt extremely frustrated. In his formal role as a police officer, the investigation would have remained active and pursued until detection.

Chapter Seventeen

The Connection

Was the assassination of James Whitehead about to be linked to a second murder committed in the nearby county of Hampshire?

Uninvited visitors rarely called at the remote country house. The front door had been opened by the sole occupant in expectation of the postman with the early morning delivery. Eye contact was brief. The owner of the house expressed annoyance at the sight of the figure standing on the doorstep.

"Who the hell are you?"

"Your executioner," replied the stranger.

He was dressed in a full white forensic suit with the hood up and wearing disposable blue latex gloves. The calm voice was somewhat muffled from behind the surgical face mask.

Without further explanation, there was a dull thud and a single bullet entered the victim's forehead. With eyes open wide and face frozen in shock, he slumped to his knees. For a moment, he tasted cordite on his lips before falling backwards onto the cold marble floor. He was dead. The killing had been carefully planned and executed with clinical efficiency.

Charles Moorland, forty-eight years old convicted drug dealer and an armed robber, laid motionless in the hallway of his country house. A man of little formal education, he was ruthless in his quest for wealth, power and respect. Usually, he was the one who inflicted fear but now he was the helpless victim.

In his youth he had served time in prison but had quickly learned the art of not getting caught and, if he did, he never admitted his guilt even when police told him they had him 'bang to rights'.

He was high on the police list of persistent professional criminals and accepted that, on occasions, he would be arrested and charged. However, the secret was to stay silent: never admit anything and let his expensive 'Brief' do the talking. In twenty-years, this philosophy had served him well. In that time, he had not been convicted of any crime and took dark pleasure in outwitting the police. He considered, he knew more about police surveillance techniques than most of the young detectives deployed against him.

Clarence Lodge, the large detached house standing in its own gated grounds, was shielded from the quiet country lane by tall cedar trees. For several weeks, the house and surrounding area had been under regular surveillance by the killer.

The day of the killing had been carefully chosen. Moorland was at home alone. His young wife had left for London ten minutes earlier in her silver BMW car and would not be home until the evening. She would be the first to find his body.

After the shooting, the killer calmly stepped forward and pulled the solid oak door closed. He then bent down and picked up the single shell case from the doorstep, thus removing the only external evidence of his visit. He walked the few steps to the cover of the trees and removed his forensic suit, which he folded and placed into a soft leather shoulder bag along with the small automatic gun fitted with a silencer.

The man, walking off down the lane, did not look out of place in this affluent part of the world. He could have passed for one of the anonymous residents going about his daily life. The houses in this corner of West Hampshire were large impersonal places, where the owners did not know each other and preferred it that way.

It was a crisp autumn morning, with a light haze drifting across the local woodland and fields. The school run had been completed thirty minutes earlier. No neighbours or tradesmen were about. Their routines had been carefully monitored by the killer to ensure he was not seen.

The rural postman normally arrived at Clarence Lodge, in his small red Royal Mail van, at 9:30 am. However, on this morning, whilst parked three miles away in the village of Beaulieu, the front nearside tyre of the van had been punctured. The van was not going anywhere until it could be fixed. This inconvenience delayed deliveries. No one had noticed the country looking gentleman stab the tyre with a stiletto knife as he walked slowly past the van.

Two months earlier, Charles Moorland had stood trial for murder at the Old Bailey law courts. A thoroughly unpleasant individual. He was a career criminal with a history of violence. The charge related to the shooting of a security guard during a foiled bank robbery in Essex. A criminal of his age and wealth had no logical reason to be taking part in an armed robbery. He had planned and financed it. He did not need to take the risk, but he enjoyed the excitement and kudos of being the 'boss'. It gave him the feeling of power and respect he craved from his own kind. At the trial, the Defence had successfully argued it was mistaken identity and that the forensic evidence had been contaminated. Alleged dubious police tactics were also brought into question.

The prosecution case had been further weakened by the failure of a principal witness to attend court. Just prior to the trial, the witness had quit his job and allegedly left the UK for an unknown destination. Police considered he had suffered intimidation from Moorland's associates or, maybe, he had been permanently silenced.

This was the second time Moorland had been acquitted of murder. Three years earlier, he had knifed a man to death in a road rage incident but, with the money to buy the best defence team and a lifestyle that generated fear in all who crossed his path, he was able to walk free from the dock.

The shooting of the 'wealthy country gent' made the evening news. The Media were quick to identify Moorland and his criminal past. Residents distanced themselves from the unpleasant event and closed ranks to reporters and television crews who descended into the area. They did not know Moorland, had never spoken to him and had not seen any strangers in the neighbourhood. None was prepared to speak on camera and, without a story, the press soon disappeared.

With no witnesses and a lack of detailed forensic evidence, the initial police investigation stalled. The single bullet recovered from the head of the deceased at the post-mortem was submitted for forensic examination by ballistics experts. From the distinctive marks and striations, the laboratory suggested it had been fired from an automatic handgun, fitted with a silencer. The weapon had been manufactured in Eastern Europe and, in recent years, such guns had been illegally used in the UK by criminals. This gun was not on the National Ballistics Index as having previously been used in crime.

Motive for the killing? The list of possibilities was endless. Moorland had embarked on a life of crime at the age of fifteen years and had made enemies at every stage of his violent career. Many wished him dead and rejoiced at his passing. None was prepared to speak to the police, even when a twenty-thousand-pound reward was offered.

With no identified suspect or positive line of enquiry, and with the Media showing no sympathy towards the victim, the investigation team was reduced in size. The Hampshire Police Major Crime Team was undertaking the murder investigation using the computerised Home Office Large Major Enquiry System, known as HOLMES2. This was the information technology system used by UK police to investigate major incidents.

All information and intelligence gleaned from the investigation, was meticulously entered into HOLMES2 and cross checked with all available UK police data bases. This included names, addresses and telephone numbers taken from the diaries and paperwork of the deceased.

His so-called 'friends or associates' might view each other with suspicion but were in no hurry to assist the police to identify a killer. They would use the opportunity to take over the more lucrative elements of his criminal activities. Few attended his funeral and even less mourned his death.

Mrs Amy Moorland had found the body of her husband when she returned home. She had immediately dialled 999 to call the emergency services. She was only one, of the few people, willing to assist the police and, back at the police station, made a full written witness statement outlining her discovery of the body and their life together.

She acknowledged he had been a ruthless individual in his dealings with criminal associates but stated she rarely met with these people and he never discussed his criminal dealings with her. She did not have any names to give to the police and had no idea who may have arranged his murder.

Amy had married Moorland ten years earlier. She was attractive and ten years younger than him. When they met, she was broke, working behind the bar of a shabby public house in the dockside area of Gravesend and living in a run-down first floor flat. She saw him as a meal ticket to a better life. He displayed all the attributes of a hard-nosed criminal, but he always had plenty of cash and in the beginning treated her as a lady. She was happy to tell the police her story.

She enjoyed the luxury the proceeds of crime had brought, but over the years she longed for more. "Charlie" had continued to associate with the same low life he had known from his youth. He had no real friends, only criminal associates. Holidays were only ever taken at their holiday villa in Paphos, on the southwest coast of Cyprus. Moorland would only visit once, maybe twice, each year for a short stay. Increasingly, Amy would spend the long Summer months there on her own. Many villas in the area were owned by fellow criminals from the UK. Their principal activity was drinking and discussing crime or playing golf at the local club run by a well-known UK criminal. The group was not welcomed in polite society within the expat community.

Moorland had always been ill at ease in social company where he could not dominate or control. He enjoyed the company of young prostitutes. Paying for sex excited him and gave him a feeling of power and gratification. His actions repulsed Amy. They no longer enjoyed sex together but, in her words, she was a 'survivor' and he was her 'bank'.

He avoided attending the theatre or any cultural event or eating out at classy restaurants. Despite his wealth, he felt an inner sense of inadequacy at such places, which would quickly develop into aggression. It took him back to being the fifteen-year-old illiterate youth who at school was laughed at by the English teacher for his inability to read out loud even the simplest passages from the set text books. Embarrassment and humiliation would never again be part of his world.

Amy with her good looks, expensive clothing and flirtatious, but practiced, reserved manners fitted well into the society to which she aspired. She acknowledged, she would not mourn his death or pursue to have his killer caught. An arrest and subsequent prosecution would only bring more unwanted publicity. Now she would inherit his money, about fifteen million pounds, revert to her maiden name and quietly reinvent herself as a respectable wealthy single woman.

It was late in the evening, and Lawson was still his office at London HQ typing up reports. Mark Holloway was also seated in the office with him. Jane Rigby appeared in the doorway, looked at Lawson and smiled.

"I think you may have your wish to continue the Operation Dismount investigation: the assassination of James Whitehead."

Jane sat down to explain the position: "The Hampshire Major Crime Team is conducting a murder investigation into the apparent 'execution' of a local professional villain called Charles Moorland. He was British, lived within the New

Forest and had a holiday villa in Cyprus. Following his death, paperwork seized from his home by police with names and addresses etc, was searched against PNC (Police National Computer) records and identified an interesting match. The name of James Whitehead and his Sussex home address were found in a notebook owned by Moorland. At this stage, the reasons for the connection are not known. The Senior Investigating Officer (SIO) for the Hampshire murder investigation has been made aware of the MI5 interest, but not given details or reasons. Jane requested that Lawson and Holloway undertake discreet enquiries.

"In recent years, Cyprus has become the favoured destination for billionaire Russian oligarchs with many taking up residence in palatial villas. The country has gained much wealth, by encouraging vast investment in their banking sector and in property development. Cyprus is a member of the European Union. The government has raised billions of pounds by allowing the super-rich to acquire EU passports under a controversial 'golden visa' scheme by providing them with citizenship. Then granting them the right to live and work throughout Europe in exchange for cash investments. This is one of the routes used by Russians to gain a foothold in the UK and transfer vast wealth into London's financial banking institutions and buy into the property and business markets. For this reason, the British Secret Intelligence Service (MI6) has agents operating within Cyprus to ensure the Foreign Office and other government departments have current intelligence on the activities of such people and their methods of channelling vast amounts of cash into the UK."

Lawson and Holloway considered the relevant facts:

- The dead man known as Whitehead was a 'failed' Russian assassin.
- His true identity remains unknown.
- He was murdered by a poisonous injection. His killer was Russian.
- He was ex-KGB and had connections with Russian organised crime and the pursuit of billionaire oligarchs.
- Moorland was British.
- His true identity is known.
- He was murdered by shooting. The gun used was manufactured in Eastern Europe.
- His lifestyle revolved around criminal activity and acquiring wealth.
- Both men were targeted and murdered by unidentified assailants.
- They lived within sixty miles of each other.
- Both had connections with Cyprus.
- Moorland had written in his notebook Whitehead's name and address.

Both lifestyles strongly indicated no developed friendships, but only associates involved in criminal activity. Did they ever meet? Was Whitehead aware of Moorland having his details? Could the Cyprus connection prove the vital link? Does Amy Moorland know more than she is telling the police?

Lawson commented, "The reason Whitehead was assassinated has been established, although the identity of the killer remains unknown. The reason why Moorland was 'executed' has not been established, although it appears gangland related."

Lawson typed up his assessment and through government classified channels, sent out enquiries to be undertaken. His initial main thrust would be to delve into the background of Charles Moorland and his wife Amy.

MI6 agents working in Cyprus were the first to report back with significant intelligence. For the previous four months, whilst living at their holiday villa without her husband, Amy had engaged in a sexual relationship with a Russian exile called Alexander. He was ex-KGB and operated as a "bodyguard come enforcer" to the billionaire oligarch set.

It was said Alexander had instigated the relationship. In recent months, Amy had confided to female friends on the island that she 'hated' her husband but needed his money to continue with her lifestyle.

Special Branch also reported back with interesting intelligence. Extensive research had been undertaken using ANPR to check on cars travelling from London along the M3 into the New Forest, two hours before the shooting of Moorland. Plus, similar research was undertaken for two hours after the shooting on cars travelling in the opposite direction. The exercise collated a list of cars that within this time slot that had travelled to and then from the New Forest. Several were of interest and required further analysis.

One car stood out. It was a white coloured VW hire car. On completing its journey, it had parked at a designated parking area within Heathrow Airport. CCTV cameras had picked out the man leaving the car and, on camera, he had been followed entering the departure terminal and catching a direct flight to Moscow. He had checked-in using a UK passport, but subsequent checks had identified it was not genuine. Further checks are ongoing. The hire car had been seized by SB and was to undergo forensic examination.

So, an early assessment would indicate Moorland was also targeted and killed by a Russian based operative. But why?

With Amy still in the UK, and at the request of Lawson, the MI6 agents in Cyprus undertook a covert operation to force an entry into her villa in Paphos.

Two agents entered the single storey villa posing as cleaners. A third agent remained in a parked van as a lookout, remaining in radio control with his two colleagues. Wearing protective clothing and latex gloves, a thorough and forensic search of the building was undertaken. DNA swabs were taken from the bathroom, toothbrushes and hairbrushes.

The wall safe was opened using technical equipment and its contents and documents photographed. Nine hundred and fifty thousand pounds in new English currency notes was found lodged in the safe. The money was photographed and left in situ. A hidden miniature listening device was fitted into a wall socket of the villa. The building was secured and the team left.

Lawson considered it was time to interview Amy Moorland. Since the murder, she had been staying at a nearby hotel in Brocklehurst. Lawson and Holloway arrived unannounced just after lunchtime. She was sitting alone in the conservatory reading a magazine. She did not ask to be shown their identity and assumed it to be a routine chat by CID officers following the shooting.

He had a copy of the witness statement she had made to the police and, over a cup of coffee, gently went through the facts with her, asking some additional questions. Amy remained calm and relaxed. Again, she denied knowing any details about her husband's criminal activities or associates, but readily acknowledged he was a "professional and successful criminal". Likewise, she had no qualms about acknowledging she did not love him.

Without changing the tone of his gentle questioning, he calmly asked: "When was the last time you spoke with Alexander?"

Amy sat back in her chair and looked straight at Lawson but did not speak.

"Shall I repeat the question?"

Again, no reply.

Lawson continued: "Your husband was murdered in a most targeted and brutal manner, so it is natural enquiries need to be undertaken in the UK, Cyprus and elsewhere. We now know about Alexander and your relationship with him. Please tell me what you know about him."

Amy replied: "He's Russian. An extraordinarily rich Russian. His holiday villa is close to mine. I love him and we have talked about a future together. And before you ask, long before Charles was killed, I had intended to divorce him, but only when it was financially right for me to do so."

"Could that be a motive for killing him?" Lawson enquired.

Amy displayed much anger: "No, no Alexander had nothing to do with it. It was probably down to someone he'd crossed over a bent business deal."

"So, when in Cyprus, does Alexander do any work?" Asked Lawson.

"No, it's his holiday retreat. He relaxes and goes about with his Russian friends."

"Are they all rich?"

"Yes, they are all billionaires or at least multimillionaires."

"And Alexander. Billionaire or multimillionaire?" Asked Lawson.

"Very rich. I have never asked him to count his money. He has certainly got enough to look after me." She said with a defiant smile.

Lawson thanked her for speaking with them and left.

Back in the car he outlined his observations to Holloway. He considered her 'street wise' in her pursuit for wealth but was concerned about her description of Alexander. She thought him to be a rich man, who just relaxed and enjoyed himself when visiting Cyprus. Yet, the detailed assessment from MI6 was that Alexander was a "bodyguard come enforcer" for the group of billionaire oligarchs he associated with. The discrepancy was relevant and interesting.

During the following two weeks, investigations continued using the facilities of the various police and security services, which included GCHQ. No information was forthcoming to implicate Amy in the murder.

In respect of the two murders, all enquiries supported the conclusion that both 'assassins' had departed the UK within hours of having committed the crimes. They had disappeared into the vast apparatus of the criminal organisations within the Russian State. They would never be brought to justice.

Further intelligence, which came from extremely sensitive sources and could never be made public, identified the motive behind Moorland's murder: The assassination of the last 'Mr Whitehead' effectively ended the long-term operation which had been managed from Timberland Lodge. Some months before the killing, the Russian organisation had anticipated the need to kill their operative 'Whitehead' and, thus, a replacement venue was required. The placement of Alexander into the affections of Amy Moorland was part of that process. With the killing of Charles Moorland, the organisation anticipated it would be recorded as a UK gangland related murder. Thus, clearing the way to develop Amy and her Hampshire house as the future base to continue their UK operation. Her villa in Cyprus would be an additional bonus.

In the coming months, MI5 with the other agencies would continue to develop their intelligence on the Russian criminal organisations and their spreading tentacles into Europe.

Chapter Eighteen
A Weekend Break

Back in his HQ London office, Lawson completed the case file he was working on and placed it in his personal safe, along with all other documents on his desk. It was Friday afternoon and he was looking forward to having a relaxing weekend break at his home in Petworth. He locked the safe and then locked the office door behind him. On passing Reception, he stopped to collect his personal iPhone: no personal digital or transmitting equipment was permitted within MI5 HQ.

It was now early autumn and it had been a warm dry season: the ideal time to chill out at home and exercise by chopping logs in his woodland. After catching spies, he had earned a weekend's rest! He exited the building turning right onto Millbank, which runs alongside the River Thames, and undertook a brisk twenty-minute walk to Victoria Railway Station where he caught the train to Pulborough. He then took a short taxi ride to his home address in Petworth.

Once at home, he changed into a casual shirt and jeans, poured himself a large glass of Highland Park single malt whisky (his favourite tipple) and walked out into the rear secluded garden. Before sitting down, he opened an old rusty biscuit tin, positioned on the wooden table outside, and took out a handful of seeds which he sprinkled on the grass. Almost instantly a single robin appeared and, without fear of human presence, pecked away at the seed. Clearly Lawson and the robin were known to each other and had performed this simple ritual many times: one of the simple pleasures in life.

After several minutes Lawson rose from his chair and walked across to the vegetable patch, picked up a gardening fork and dug over the soil to expose fresh wriggling earthworms. The robin hopped across the garden and gratefully began eating his 'dessert' course. Robins are relatively unafraid of people and drawn to human activity, if it is to their benefit. Male birds are noted for their overly aggressive behaviour and will fiercely attack other competitors that stray into their territory, even much larger birds. Lawson and his robin 'friend' have much in common. Another glass of whisky, listening to a Rod Stewart CD and then to bed for an early night.

Saturday morning was another warm autumn day with a clear blue sky. He was going to have a few quiet relaxing hours working in his woodland: neither switching on the radio to listen to the World news nor bothering to read the Saturday newspapers. Just a slow hot shower, followed by toast and lots of fresh coffee.

The perfect silence was broken by the bleeping of his iPhone. He took it from his trouser pocket and read the text message: 'GOOD MORNING MR NUISANCE. JUST HAPPEN TO BE VISITING WEST SUSSEX. REMEMBER I OFFERED TO TAKE YOU FOR A MEAL. FANCY TODAY? YOUR FAVOURITE MISS NASTY.'

Lawson smiled, realising it was Sally Chambers. He thought for a moment and then texted back: 'HOPE YOU

ARE NOT AGAIN UP TO YOUR SURVEILLANCE TRICKS! I'M HAVING A QUIET DAY AT HOME. FROM YOUR PREVIOUS TRAINING EXERCISE, YOU KNOW WHERE I LIVE. HOW ABOUT VISITING ME AND I'LL COOK YOU A SPECIAL LUNCH. LOOK FORWARD TO SEEING YOU SOON.' And for the added guidance of her GPS, he included his postcode.

Within the hour, Lawson heard a car on his gravel driveway approaching the house and stop. He walked towards her parked Mini Cooper and graciously, and with humour, opened the driver's door: "A surprise, but good to see you Sally." He gave her a gentle hug.

Since their initial contact, involving the infamous sting exercise during his training period with the service, he had seen her on occasions at London HQ, when she would often remind him that the offer to take him for a meal was still open. They had never actually worked together on an operation.

"What a lovely cottage set in such a tranquil setting. You must tell me about it."

"It's a two-storey detach cottage, built about 1880 as the house of the gamekeeper, when this formed part of a much larger country estate. The cottage came with twenty acres of woodland which, as a hobby, I try to manage. My late wife and I purchased it as our bolt hole, and little bit of paradise, away from the brutal World. Come in for a coffee and then I'll show you around my estate." He added with a mischievous smile.

Following coffee, from the rear garden he opened a five-bar wooden gate and they walked together into the woodland and onto a grass track. They walked slowly, as Lawson pointed out and explained some of the main features of the woodland: To the north of the woodland, are located six acres of sweet chestnut which had recently been coppiced by a professional forestry company.

In his 'woodman' enthusiastic mode he playfully explained the rotation cycle (every fifteen to twenty years) for cutting the sweet chestnut trees, which is hardwood and mainly used for stakes and making fencing. He was showing Sally the new growth when he stopped, spoke very softly, and pointed to the distance: "Look, a Roe Deer. That is a Buck (male) with a small set of antlers. Usually solitary animals, but this time of the year, expect to see them in small groups. We'll remain here for a minute." And soon after, two more deer appeared, and quickly disappeared into the undergrowth.

He explained, they roamed wild and were increasing in numbers throughout the South of England. They caused damage to new woodlands, particularly to the new tender shoots of his recently coppiced sweet chestnut woodland and it was essential to maintain, by culling, a balance of a sustainable healthy deer population: "Even in paradise, nature has to be managed, but I leave that to the professionals."

They continued walking and talking as they slowly made their way along the track, running through the centre of the woodland until they arrived at a log cabin. "One of my projects. The wood was sawn from trees grown on this woodland and built by me. And I enjoyed doing it."

The cabin measured approximately four metres square, with an open sided veranda on a raised wooden base and a sloping corrugated roof. Two old wooden Ercol rocking chairs, courtesy of eBay, were positioned on the decking area. Opposite the rocking chairs, situated in the corner of the veranda, was located a cast iron wood burning stove, fitted with a flexible stainless-steel flue that disappeared up through an opening in the corrugated roof. Lawson pointed a short distance away to a small wooden shack: "That's the compost toilet."

Lawson unlocked the padlock on the double doors leading into the main room of the cabin. The room contained a small table, on which sat a vintage brass oil lamp, two wicker chairs, a single metal framed camp bed and a dog basket in the corner.

A large white notice board was fixed to the left side wall of the cabin with colour photographs of the woodland, including its wildlife, flora and fauna, taken at different times of the day and year. There were also several photographs of a young women, clearly enjoying her relaxed and happy surroundings. Sally assumed they were photographs of his late wife. He was aware Sally was looking at them. She did not ask any questions, and he did not offer an explanation. They returned to the outer section of the cabin.

Lawson said he visited the cabin all through the year. Sometimes with his iPad as a quiet place to type up reports; sometimes to do physical work and chop logs and sometimes just to relax and enjoy his woodland surroundings. He particularly enjoyed the cold winter months, when he would sit in his rocking chair, light a blazing fire in the wood burner and, on the flat top surface, boil a kettle of water for a mug of coffee. He would often remain there into the late evening until it was dark, taking in the silence and solitude. It was in total contrast to his working environment.

With a broad grin on his face Lawson announced: "I promised to cook you a special lunch. The fun starts here."

He took from his rucksack four chopstick size lengths of wood and handed two to Sally. She appeared puzzled but was game for the experience.

"I'm going to cook a barbecue of beef burgers, fried eggs, bacon, baked beans etc. A proper woodman's lunch. But first we need to start the campfire."

They walked across to the camping area where he had set out logs for the making of a campfire. Plus, a small pile of kindle (small pieces of dry wood chippings). From a decaying log, he collected a small amount of dry moss and, in his hands, moulded it into a loosely formed ball.

He explained, in a playful tone, that Sally was required to light the fire by rubbing the two sticks together. He gave detailed instructions: "The friction will cause heat and the smouldering charcoal will ignite and drop onto the moss. Then gently blow into the ball of moss to provide more oxygen to stoke the fire. Once well alight, place the lighted moss within the pile of kindle and continue to gently blow. Then add small logs, until you have achieved a roaring campfire."

Sally did not look convinced but was willing to try and she was enjoying her fun day in the woodland.

"With your two sticks are you going to show me how it is done?" she enquired.

In a mischievous response he said: "I'm fully trained in the techniques of bushcraft. I will give you a five-minute start. Be patient. It takes practice."

Sally set to the task with enthusiasm, furiously rubbing the two sticks together. Lawson interjected: "Keep at it."

Despite much effort by Sally, the sticks would not smoulder or show the slightest sign of igniting the moss.

"Has the student given up?" asked Lawson.

"Yes, I bloody have. Now let us see you do it."

Lawson carefully laid out the kindle by the side of the bundle of small logs. He then plucked moss from a nearby tree, rolled it into a loose ball and placed it on the ground. Kneeling over the moss he began rubbing his two sticks together. Almost immediately a spark flew into the ball of moss, with a faint stream of smoke rising from it. He cupped it in his hands and gently blew into the ball. Once fully alight, he transferred the moss ball into the kindle and, bending lower, continued to blow into the fire.

Sally looked on in mocked amusement. The master had triumphed!

As Lawson got to his feet, he deliberately allowed a small cigarette lighter to fall to the ground from the palm of his left hand. He looked at Sally and gave a big boyish grin.

"And for a moment I was really impressed" exclaimed Sally with much laughter.

"The first and the most important lesson in bushcraft and in life is that, 'never expend energy unnecessarily.'" He picked up the lighter and handed it to her: "Have it as a keepsake of a lovely day together."

Together they fussed around the campfire and prepared their lunch, which was eaten from army style mess-tins as they sat together on a bale of straw. "It is truly lovely and peaceful here" commented Sally.

On completion of their lunch, and with each holding a can of beer, they strolled back to the cabin and sat on the comfortable rocking chairs. Facing out into the woodland, they watched as the sun began to sink lower in the West with its rays penetrating through the branches of the tall beech trees.

Lawson was relaxed but clearly in a quiet reflective mood. Sally asked him what he was thinking and was he happy with life?

He did not immediately answer but, for the first time, stretched across and with affection gently squeezed her hand.

"My current role has given me much to think about. To think about life and to think about me and my part in it. It is full of unknowns and contradictions. I work closely with a small team of dedicated people. We trust and rely on each other's integrity and professional ability, yet I know nothing about them personally. I know them only by their cover names and their manufactured CV's. What are their real interests or hobbies? Are they married or in relationships? What about their families? Where do they holiday? I know sod all about any of them. Recently a colleague on my team was killed on active service up in Scotland: killed, shot, murdered and yet I don't see any grieving from the service."

"And that worries you?" asked Sally.

Lawson gave a nervous smile: "If a group of red Indians came running out of this woodland and tied me upside down to that tree and interrogated me about the team members, I couldn't tell them much."

Sally smiled: "Do you get many red Indians in your woods?"

"Only a few, in the warm Summer months" he joked. "And yes, I understand and accept the reasoning: the defection or indiscretion of one individual can't collapse the 'house of cards' for the organisation. But it puts us in a strange, rather surreal World."

Sally asked: "Why do you do this job?"

"It was nothing I sought. The Service targeted and recruited me. I enjoy a good game of chess. I enjoy solving complex issues. The thought of doing a basic nine to five, Monday to Friday, job doing virtually the same thing day after day would send me crazy. That is why I joined the police. I need that challenge of never knowing what is going to greet me, when I turn up for work. And, with no form of a private income, I need a regular salary to pay the mortgage and live a fairly comfortable existence."

Sally commented: "I've noticed you never mention your late wife by name."

"That is deliberate. She is not part of my fake identity. My fake World. She remains special to me and to my real self."

"And where do you see your future?"

"You sound like a counsellor: my personal psychotherapist! Your short responses support the point I am trying to make. I am thirty-eight and moderately intelligent. I have a good class university law degree. I have enjoyed an active professional life and experienced the good, the bad and the ugly. Yet there is a barrier, a protocol of establishment secrecy, which prevents us crossing that invisible line."

Sally leaned forward and continued to gently hold his hand.

Lawson continued: "My knowledge of my team members is based mostly on my observations and assumptions. Take Jane Rigby as an example. Factually, I know nothing about her real identity, background or family. She speaks with a polished English accent and has an inner confidence and authority. She wears conservative, but expensive, clothes and always with matching accessories.

"My assessment: she comes from a well to do family, father possibly retired senior civil service or military, attended private boarding school followed by Oxford or Cambridge. In all the months I have worked with her, I can only recall two occasions in which she referred to her personal life. Once, she commented she was going to leave the office early to attend the Glyndebourne Opera House Festival and, on another occasion, I overhead her on the telephone saying, she needed to have a vet examine her horses. Just a couple of snippets about her life. It doesn't worry me unduly, but we all lead a rather strange and detached secret existence."

He continued: "Nothing is what it seems. Some poor individual somewhere around the World falls to their death from the tenth-floor hotel balcony: is it suicide or a carefully constructed assassination? Or a car crash: is it an accident or an assassination? Or a sudden death: is it a heart attack or death by poison injection?"

Sally changed the direction of his thoughts: "I noticed a dog basket in the cabin. Do you have a dog?"

"No. I'm away too much to own one. The elderly couple, who look after my house when I am away, have a lovely old English sheep dog called 'Molly' and occasionally they let me steal her for the day. When my wife was poorly, we used to joke that when she was no longer with us, I would purchase a Jack Russell dog for company and name it after my wife."

He continued: "You are good at your job. We have walked and talked as we strolled around my woodland. We have continued chatting over lunch and sitting here together, yet you haven't told me anything about yourself, nor have I much about myself."

Sally replied: "I contacted you today because I was keen to see you. So that tells you something about me. I have been with the service for ten years and neither my family nor my social friends know what I do. I often ask myself the sort of questions you have posed today.

"Recently, I attended the Old Bailey Crown Court to give evidence in a terrorism trial. I was bused in a closed van, via the back entrance and gave evidence standing in the witness box from behind a screen. I did not enjoy that experience: I was part of the prosecution process but not a part of the reality, and I could not even tell my family about it. I feel 'I'm always present, but never there' and that is the record of my life."

Lawson said, "Let me tell you a story. Many months back, I met an attractive young lady called Lucy standing by her broken-down Land Rover. She seemed genuine and friendly. She told me about her family home in West Yorkshire, her private education, how she had travelled the World after university and how she now felt it was time to settle done. I was attracted by her charm. Then I find it was all bollocks. Total bollocks."

Sally smiled, "I was hoping you had forgiven me. Honestly, I am charming."

Lawson responded, "Initially, I was taken in by the charms of a girl called Lucy, who then reappears as Sally and charms me a little more. But that is only your cover name. The World is mad or is it just me."

"No, you and me, and I'm sure many of our colleagues feel the same way. Last month, I attended a colleague's retirement after thirty years with the service. Cannot call her a friend because I only knew her by her cover identity. Saying farewell after thirty years of loyal service and no photographs allowed. She left the building, gave in her security pass, and will never be allowed back in to visit or share a coffee."

"So, what of your future?" asked Lawson.

"Definitely not a thirty-year girl. I've been with the service for ten years and enjoy the buzz of being busy and important but, when I am off-duty and my cover identity documents are safely put in my home safe, I feel lonely and isolated."

After a pause Sally continued: "You bastard, or should I say thank you, I've never before told that to anyone."

The pair was beginning to form an attachment for each other.

It was time to leave. Lawson secured the doors to the cabin then walked across to the still glowing campfire. He kicked the embers to the centre of the fire to ensure it was safe to burn itself out. He took Sally's hand and slowly walked back along the grass track to his cottage.

"I've enjoyed our day together. In truth, we know very little about each other, but I feel we have much in common, and I'm going to ask you out for a proper date."

Sally stopped, smiled and hugged his arm.

"The answer is yes. That would take us into the realms of a likely relationship, requiring notification in triplicate to London HQ."

Before they parted, Lawson informed Sally that the service had made a formal approach for him to become a permanent member of the organisation beyond his two-year secondment. He had not given a reply. He had much to consider and, jokingly, said that if he returned to the role of a police officer Sally would have to know his true identify. Their future could prove interesting.

THE END